MOVING
FAR
AWAY

Esther Abbott
II Cor. 9:8

ESTHER ABBOTT

MOVING
FAR
AWAY

A FAMILY IN TRANSITION

TATE PUBLISHING
AND ENTERPRISES, LLC

Published by Tate Publishing & Enterprises, LLC
127 E. Trade Center Terrace | Mustang, Oklahoma 73064 USA
1.888.361.9473 | www.tatepublishing.com

Tate Publishing is committed to excellence in the publishing industry. The company reflects the philosophy established by the founders, based on Psalm 68:11,
"The Lord gave the word and great was the company of those who published it."

Book design copyright © 2014 by Tate Publishing, LLC. All rights reserved.
Cover design by Anne Gatillo
Interior design by Gram Telen
Illustrations by Esther Abbott, Mica L. Fehr and Nikki Abbott
Cover painting by Nikki Abbott

Published in the United States of America

ISBN: 978-1-62854-143-4
Fiction / Family Life
Fiction / Christian / General
13.12.04

DEDICATION

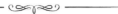

To all the Filipino people who work for and with expatriate missionaries, helping us learn the language and culture and patiently putting up with our mistakes.

ACKNOWLEDGEMENTS

Thank you to my coworkers in the Philippines, especially Don, who encouraged us to write.

Thank you to the Institute of Children's Literature, whose course introduced me to the basics of writing, and to my teacher Norma Jean who patiently worked with me and challenged me to keep going.

Thank you to my husband, Jack, for your support, your suggestions and your invaluable help in formatting my manuscript for submission.

Thank you to my daughter-in-law Kay for your knowledgeable input and tireless technical help on the artwork for this book.

Thank you to the staff at Tate Publishing for your encouragement and for working with me to see this book published.

Thank you to my Lord and Savior Jesus Christ, whose ways are right and whose timing is perfect.

CONTENTS

———— ❧ ————

INTRODUCTION

———— ❧❦❧ ————

FILIPINO CHARACTERS, PRONUNCIATION AND CULTURE

Pronunciation key: ā pay, ä father, ē bee, ī pie, ō toe, ōō boot, oi noise.

Stressed syllables are preceded by a stress mark or are italicized.

Tagalog (tä-'gä-lōg) (tah-*gah*-low g) Basis for the Philippine national language.

Filipino family living across the street from Jenny and her family in the province:

Angel (pronounced as in English) is the younger sister. She accepts her hardships as part of life.

Ate Ana ('ä-tä 'ä-nä) (*ah*-tay *ah*-nah) *Ate* is used for older sisters and female relatives, and for respected females in the same generation as the speaker. *Ate* Ana is almost sixteen and in her last year of school.

Inay (ē-'nī) (ee-*nigh*) *Inay* means mother. She leaves her family in the care of relatives to work abroad.

Tatay ('tä-tī) (*tah*-tie) *Tatay* means father. He is a *tricycle* driver. His income doesn't meet all the family's needs even though he works long hours.

tricycle (trī-sē-'kāl) (try-see-*kel**) A *tricycle*—often called *trike* (trike*) in the Philippines—is a motorcycle with covered sidecar used as public transportation.

Totoy ('tō-toi) (*toe*-toy) *Totoy* means baby brother or youngest brother.

Kuya Jun ('kōō-yä jōōn) (*coo*-yah june) *Kuya* is used for older brothers and male relatives, and for respected males in the same generation as the speaker. *Kuya* Jun is an unmarried oldest brother, who sometimes stays at home and sometimes elsewhere. He occasionally helps with family needs.

Nanay ('nä-nī) (*nah*-nigh) *Nanay* means mother and in some places grandmother. It is also a term of respect for an elderly lady. She, Angel's grandmother, lives with the family and has a *sari-sari* store in front of their small home. Although in poor health, she runs the home and cares for the children while her daughter is abroad.

sari-sari ('sä-rē-'sä-rē) (*sah*-ree *sah*-ree*) store. *Sari-sari* means a little of this and that, a variety.

Tiyo Romy ('tē-yō 'rō-mē) (*tee*-yo *row*-mee) *Tiyo* means uncle.

Tiya Nene ('tē-yä 'nä-nä) (*tee*-yah *nay*-nay) *Tiya* means aunt.

*In *Tagalog* the letter *R* is pronounced something like the *D* in *rider*.

Missionary family's maid or main house help:

Ka Tala (kä 'tä-lä) (kah *tah*-lah) *Ka* used with the first name is a term of respect for an elder. She is a Christian lady hired as a maid by Jenny's parents. She has worked for other missionaries and explains Filipino culture to the family. *Ka* Tala is a distant relative of Angel's father.

In the Philippines, maids—house helpers—replace modern conveniences in the US. Having a maid is the cultural way to handle household chores, shopping and childcare. Many Filipino families have maids, often a young relative or someone from another island. They usually live with the family and are part of the family, but everybody knows what is expected. Maids of missionaries often commute and are treated as employees. The relationship between missionaries and maids is difficult for Americans to understand and takes patience and experience on both sides to make it work, but maids can be a great blessing and aid to the work of missions.

PACKING

─────── ❧ ───────

Before, eight-year-old Jenny thought moving to a new country would be exciting, but not now. Her lips quivered and tears filled her brown eyes. She stared at the square cardboard packing box in the middle of her bedroom floor and at the piles heaped around it.

"Here are the new clothes we bought yesterday," Jenny's mom said, coming into her room and handing her a pile of shorts and tops. "Put them in your box, please."

"How can I get everything I want to take into this one dumb box? It's not fair."

"Don't talk like that, Jenny," Mom commanded. "Oh, dear," she went on, "I still need to trim your bangs. Push your hair out of your eyes. And, Jenny..." Mom paused. Jenny slowly reached up and pushed her bangs to the side. She waited. Was her mom ever going to finish her sentence? Finally, she continued, "It's only half an hour until Tara expects you over at her house. What have you been doing all morning?" Then, without waiting for Jenny to answer, her mom hurried out the door.

"Mom certainly isn't very nice lately," Jenny said quietly to Charlotte who sat motionless in her rocking chair next to the box. Jenny wished she had long auburn curls like Charlotte's instead of shortish, straightish hair. And what color was hers anyway? Was it blond? Was it light brown? Charlotte was so beautiful. But mostly, Jenny loved Charlotte because she knew if she was real, and not just a doll, she would understand perfectly. Right now, her lovely greenish eyes looked sad. Her half-smiling mouth seemed to say, "Jenny, I am truly sorry. I know it's not fair."

She would not leave Charlotte behind; even if Mom said her porcelain arms and legs might break on the long trip to the Philippines. Jenny took her set of *Little House* books back out of the packing box. She lovingly wrapped Charlotte in the new shorts and tops, still warm from the dryer, and laid her carefully in the box. "I love you," Jenny whispered. "I will pack my music box from Grandma right next to you, because it's my next favorite thing besides you."

Tears blurred the delicately carved wooden music box as she tucked it in the folds of Charlotte's ruffled dress. "It's unbreakable," Grandma had said. "It weighs almost nothing and is so small it won't take up much space. And whenever you wind it up and listen to the song, you'll remember I love you." Jenny remembered that once, long ago, Grandma had taught missionary children in the Philippines. She'd often helped her with homeschooling, too, but no more seeing Grandma for four years. A wave of sickness sloshed around in her empty stomach. How could she bear it?

And how could she bear not getting to go to the Christian school next year? It was to be her first year in a real school. She was counting on having the same, wonderful third-grade teacher her best friend, Tara, had had this year. One time Mrs. Brown invited Jenny to come to school to tell the children about her parents' plan to be missionaries in the Philippines.

Mrs. Brown had turned her globe around to the opposite side from the United States. She showed the children small islands not far from the huge country of China. Mrs. Brown said, "When it is daytime here, it is nighttime in the Philippines. And when it is daytime there, it is nighttime here." She'd slowly turned the globe so the bright spring sunshine coming through the classroom window shone on the Philippine Islands, while the United States on the opposite side was in the shadow.

"What are you doing, Jenny?" Mom called.

What could she say? Daydreaming?

"Jenny."

"I'm packing," Jenny called, looking at the almost full box. It had been almost full all morning.

A week ago, her mother had set the empty box down on the floor of her bedroom and said, "You can take the things that will fit in here. Be sure you really want them," she'd added.

Well, nothing would fit, and she wanted everything. How to decide? What would she really want when she was way over there? She didn't know. The first time she'd packed the box Mom had come in and said, "Don't take that stuff. There'll be stores over there. Take what is really special to you."

Jenny looked at the things still scattered on her bedroom floor. "What is really special to me," she said out loud, "is Froggie." Froggie had slept on her bed even before she could remember. He was truly special. She picked up her dear, tattered, green Froggie and put him on top of the box.

Then Jenny walked out into the living room. She stepped between falling-over piles lying on the carpet. Her mom was kneeling by one of the boxes that lined the wall where her piano once stood. She was lifting out a pile of photo albums and putting in a pile of towels. *Mom doesn't seem to know what to pack either,* Jenny thought.

Jenny attempted a conversation. "It's a good thing those people who bought our living room furniture and your piano picked them up already," she said. "Now you have lots of space to organize your packing." *Organize* was a word her mom liked to use, but she hadn't seemed to hear Jenny. She was rearranging different heaps on the floor and mumbling to herself. *Mom talked to herself an awful lot lately,* Jenny thought.

"Help me carry these back into David's room." Jenny supposed her mom was speaking to her now, though she hadn't even looked up. Two-year-old David's room, or his old room, was where they were keeping all the things they planned to put into storage. The people who'd bought his bed had picked it up last week, so he'd been sleeping on the floor in their parents' room. Mom handed Jenny the heavy photo albums.

"You aren't going to take these?" Jenny asked, amazed. Just last night she'd heard her mom telling her dad that she definitely would not leave them behind.

"No. I won't be taking them," her mother answered very softly. "Oh," Mom added. "Put these in your box please, Jenny." She laid a pair of new tennis shoes on the albums.

"How?"

"Somehow."

The tennis shoes were huge. She'd probably only go barefoot in the Philippines anyway. "I won't need these," Jenny whined.

Jenny thumped the albums down on the floor in David's room and shuffled slowly back to her room. This afternoon, people would be coming to take away her furniture. She ached from her head to her toes with longing for everything just to be a dream. She'd wake up soon, and it would all be the same as always before.

"Dumb packing box!" she muttered. She barely squeezed in one shoe, pushing Froggie almost over the edge. But there wasn't another tiny hole of emptiness anywhere.

"Dad is ready to tape up your box," Mom said, swooping through the door. "And it's time for you to go." Then she spotted Froggie. "Oh, Jenny, we don't have room for that old frog."

Hurt and sadness and anger prickled inside Jenny. She couldn't even talk. She snatched up Froggie by his floppy back legs and hurled him under her bed. His soft body thumped against the floor.

She knew she'd be punished for that, but she didn't care. But what if Mom wouldn't let her go to Tara's now?

LEAVING

Jenny fixed her eyes on the horrid tennis shoes taking Froggie's place in her box. She would never wear those shoes, she promised herself. Her eyes filled with tears for the third time that morning. Everything was quiet. She waited.

Why wasn't her mom saying anything? Jenny took a deep breath and slowly looked sideways toward the door where her mom stood. She couldn't figure out the look on her face. It wasn't the look Mom usually had when she was going to punish her. "Run along, Jenny," Mom said finally. "Have a great time with the girls."

Jumping up, Jenny flung her arms around her mom's neck then was out the door.

She would have a great time! Tara had invited Connie and Rachel, too. The girls took the special lunch packed for them and headed to their favorite place. They sat together on a big blanket by the creek behind Tara's house and ate their lunch. After eating, the four of them took turns pushing each other in the two swings Tara's dad had put up for them nearby. Then they took off their shoes and walked along the edge of the creek. The soft mud squished up between their toes. They squealed and screamed. After rinsing their feet in the cold creek water, they lay down side by side on the blanket. "Tell us what it will be like in the Philippines," the girls begged.

"I only know a little," Jenny began. "Missionaries showed us slides one night. They went snorkeling in the ocean. The sand on the beach was whitest white, and the ocean was bluest blue. Palm trees and little stick houses with thatched roofs were on the beach."

"Will you live in a house like that?" Tara asked, wide-eyed.

Jenny hadn't thought of that until now. "I guess so," she answered.

"Are the people over there *natives*?" Connie wondered.

"They're Filipinos." Jenny wasn't exactly sure if they were *natives*. "Mostly," she continued, "I will play with my very own puppy Mom and Dad promised I could have when we get there."

"Fun." Tara hugged Jenny. "I know you'll love it. When our dog was a puppy, it was the cutest thing." They all giggled.

They sang silly songs and talked and laughed until they heard Tara's mom calling. "Your mother says you need to come home now, Jenny."

The girls hugged each other. "We'll never forget you," Connie said.

"Be sure to write us the minute you get there," added Rachel.

"We'll always be best friends forever, even if you're living on the other side of the world," said Tara. Arm in arm, the three girls walked Jenny back to her house for the last time.

It had been a great time. How could she ever live without her friends? She needed them. They were the best friends in the whole world.

Pastor and his wife were Mom and Dad's best friends. Tonight, their family was going to the pastor's for supper. They would sleep there, too. Then they would get up at four o'clock in the morning to go to the airport.

Jenny went up the steps into her house and headed toward her room to get ready. Hurrying through the doorway, she came to a sudden stop, confused. Her room was absolutely bare. Her bed. Gone. Her dresser, her chair, her pink-checked curtains. All gone. The box she'd packed. Gone. Froggie. Gone. The closet. Totally empty. Jenny sank to the floor and burst into tears. She didn't know what to do. She wasn't angry. She wasn't anything. She, too, was just…empty.

Above her sobs she heard her mom's voice. "I feel like the rug is being pulled out from under my feet," she was saying as she hurried past Jenny's bedroom door. Then she stopped, turned around and came back.

"Oh, hi Dear, I didn't know you were home," Mom said in a more cheerful voice.

"Everything's gone," Jenny wailed.

Mom knelt down beside her and handed her a tissue. "I'm sorry, Jenny. I know just how you feel. But we did ask the people who bought your furniture to wait to pick it up our last day here, remember?"

Mom didn't understand. She just kept talking. "Pastor is here with the church van," she continued, standing up. "He and Dad are loading up our boxes and suitcases. He says his wife has made a special supper for us." Her mom patted her on the head and turned toward the door. "I have to go see about something. Are you OK?"

No, she wasn't OK, but she stopped sobbing.

At Pastor's house it was so much fun that Jenny hardly remembered they were leaving until she heard her dad say, "Time to bed down, kids. Four a.m. will come early."

Jenny felt like she'd just fallen asleep when she heard her mom's voice. "Wake up, Jenny."

It was dark and cold. Jenny was shaking as she pulled on the clothes her mom had laid on the bed. Davy was jumping around singing, "Go airpane 'day. Go airpane 'day." Mom struggled to dress him.

It was just getting light when they pulled up in front of the airport and unloaded their things onto the sidewalk. Jenny looked for her box. She couldn't see it. Had it been left behind by mistake with the boxes going to storage? Charlotte. Grandma's music box.

Jenny started to ask about it, but just then a man in a uniform came with a large cart. He and Dad put the boxes and suitcases on it and disappeared inside the airport. Jenny clung to Pastor's wife's hand. She felt very small and her backpack was getting heavy. They walked a long, long ways. Sometimes, they stepped onto a black floor that moved them along magically without their having to walk. And so many people! Once, she saw several pretty flight attendants pulling their suitcases on two-wheeled carts behind them.

Finally, they came to a room of chairs. At last she could take off her backpack and sit down. Her legs ached. Her stomach hurt. "Mom, we forgot to eat breakfast," she said, looking up at her mom. Mom didn't seem to hear. She kept shifting David from one hip to the other and looking around. Now she was smiling. Dad was coming. Soon they were hugging and saying good-bye to the pastor and his wife. Pastor prayed. Then they walked down a slanting hall, around a turn, and through a door into another room lined with small windows and filled with rows of tall seats.

Her dad buckled her in. Was this the airplane? Somehow, without ever seeing it, was she already on it? She looked out the window and could see other huge planes. One was backing slowly away from the building. Jenny wanted to run back into the airport, back to her home, back to her friends, back to Charlotte and Froggie. Then she remembered. Her room was empty. Charlotte was gone. She wanted them. She just wanted…something.

ARRIVING

———— ◦~◦~◦ ————

Engines started roaring louder and louder. The plane began rushing along the runway. Jenny felt herself being pushed back against the soft seat. Stretching forward as far as she could in her seat belt, she pressed her head against the window. Trees and houses below were shrinking. Cars, looking like toys, moved along tiny streets. She could see the whole city. Fluffy white clouds floated by. She became a giant bird gliding in the blue sky high above the world.

"Here comes our breakfast," Mom said, her voice interrupting Jenny's imagination.

"Will we eat right here?" Jenny asked, remembering the time she'd tried to hold a plate on her lap at a potluck dinner, and how it had dumped over on the floor right in front of everyone.

Mom reached over and unfolded a tray from the back of the seat in front of her. Perfect. And one was in front of Mom and another in front of David, who was strapped into the seat on the other side of Mom. Jenny watched her dad across the aisle pulling down his tray.

Flight attendants pushed a big cart along the aisle. As they passed out food trays, one of the ladies smiled at Jenny and asked, "Are you doing OK?"

"Yes. Fine, thank you," she answered, smiling back. Jenny uncovered a plate of bacon, eggs and toast. Beside the toast was a little container of jelly. Under another plastic lid was a muffin and beside it, a wrapped square of butter. Another covered plastic dish held strawberries.

Mom passed her a fat, see-through cup of juice, then picked up a package from beside Jenny's plate and tore off the end. "This is your silverware and napkin. Pray by yourself and go ahead. Try not to spill anything, Jenny. I have to help Davy. He's into everything." Eating on the plane was fun. After the pretty flight attendants cleared away all the food trays, Mom stood up and took her carry-on from a cupboard above their heads. She pulled out a flat paper bag. "Here are things Pastor's wife sent along for you to do on the plane, Jenny," she said. Pastor's wife was like Charlotte, thought Jenny. She knew exactly what she liked. *Oh, wherever are Charlotte…and poor, poor Froggie?*

Jenny didn't know flying would take so long. She worked on the activity books. She ate more meals from trays filled with covered plastic dishes and cute little packages. At one of the airports where they landed, they all got off the plane and went inside for a while. After taking off again, Jenny curled up on a pillow and snuggled under a blanket. She didn't know if it was morning or night. Sometimes she wasn't sure if she was asleep or awake. Always the hum of the airplane's engines buzzed in her head.

"Look out your window, Jenny," Mom's voice came through the engine noise.

She had already looked and looked and looked. It was getting boring. Billowy clouds. Blue-green ocean far, far, far beyond. It was all topsy-turvy. Instead of looking up to see the clouds, she looked down.

Then she saw what Mom was seeing. Green and brown land outlined in white on a blue ocean. It looked like what was called a relief map in Dad's atlas. Jenny's stomach flip-flopped with excitement. "Is that the Philippines, Mom?" She didn't need to ask, really. She knew it.

"I remember the first time I saw the Philippines," Mom said.

"Why did you stay for only one year, Mom?" Jenny asked, still looking down at the big islands.

"My parents, Grandma and Grandpa, weren't missionaries like we are, Jenny. They came for one year to teach missionary children while their regular teachers were on furlough."

"Will I go to the Christian school?" Jenny asked, looking at her mom.

"Yes, but I plan to homeschool you until we're used to living here."

So she would get to go to a real school after all! Jenny looked out the window again. The white outline was clearer now, and she could see waves breaking against the sandy beaches. Toy boats bobbed on the ocean. Here and there colorful coral reefs showed through the clear water. She would love snorkeling!

Suddenly, she could no longer see the ocean. Below them was a giant patchwork quilt. Green squares, brown squares, and greenish, bluish, whitish squares.

Smoke was rising from dark spots on some of the brown squares.

"Rice paddies," Mom said, as she leaned across Jenny to look down. "The brown ones are already harvested and the rice hulls are being burned. The green ones are rice that's growing, and the others have just been flooded for planting."

Soon Jenny felt the little bump the airplane wheels made on the runway. The plane had touched down. Filipinos on the plane clapped and cheered. As they taxied past rice paddies toward the airport, she saw jumbo jets parked next to the big building. Jenny felt confused. Could this really be the Philippines? This looked like the airport back home. Or maybe she'd forgotten. Home seemed so far away and so long ago. Was she really on the other side of the world?

Like in the other airports, Jenny carried her backpack and held tightly to Mom's hand. They trudged up the long, narrow, winding corridor into the terminal. She felt very warm.

A Filipino lady next to them in line pinched David's cheek. He drew back with a cry and buried his head in Daddy's neck. The lady smiled at Jenny. "Is this your first time to visit the Philippines?" she asked. Jenny buried her face in Mom's side. Nobody would pinch her cheeks.

They collected their suitcases and boxes from the baggage area, put them on two carts, and stood in more lines. Finally outside the terminal, they found a missionary waiting for them. He began helping Jenny's dad load everything into a van. Jenny wondered what she would do without Charlotte if her box had been forgotten. But there was the promised puppy. A tingle of excitement rippled through her body. She couldn't wait to hold her soft, cuddly little puppy.

Dad lifted off her backpack. Sweat ran down his forehead and dripped off the end of his nose. Jenny was sweating, too. Horns honked. Taxi drivers on the street and people coming out of the airport called to one another. Cars started and stopped. Exhaust fumes choked her. She could barely breathe. How thankful she was to climb inside the van!

The missionary started slowly pulling away from the airport. "Welcome to Manila," he said, steering between the tangles of vehicles.

Buildings with open-front stores lined the streets. Cars and buses and jeeps filled the streets. Men and women, and even little kids, walked back and forth between lanes of traffic that were slowing down for a red light. They held up trays of cigarettes and candy. The missionary bought a handful of what looked like pieces of candy wrapped in green paper. "These are pretty good," he said, passing them around. The hard thing tasted cool in Jenny's hot mouth, something like a cough drop, but different.

At the stoplight, crowds of people moved onto the street like a giant wave. "What a sea of people!" Mom exclaimed.

So, Jenny thought, *this is the kind of sea it is after all.* Had she just imagined wide, blue oceans and peaceful, sandy beaches? This did not seem one bit like an island.

Horns honked. Motors roared. Black smoke billowed out behind buses.

Then Jenny saw something else she had never imagined. Golden arches?

"How about lunch at McDonald's before we go to the mission home? Are you hungry?" asked the missionary. Jenny wasn't hungry. It seemed like they had eaten a hundred meals on the plane...but McDonald's, in the Philippines?

At the door a smiling man in a dark blue uniform greeted them. As he held open the door, Jenny drew back, clinging to her mom. Strapped over the man's shoulder was a big gun. Was it real? What was going to happen? But the missionary didn't seem to notice. He led them inside to wait by a table where people were finishing their meal. Like the streets, McDonald's, too, was full of people. But the air-conditioning felt wonderful.

After slipping to the back of their booth, Jenny first dared to look around. It was McDonald's for sure. It was the same as home, but different. What was different? She looked quickly back at the uniformed man. He was opening the door for everyone coming in or going out. His face was friendly. He still held the big gun. Jenny nibbled a few fries and sipped her cold Sprite.

Outside the door, as they were leaving, Jenny saw a bony dog licking up bits and pieces of food scraps from the sidewalk. She ached to see her darling puppy. No one had told her what it might look like. She knew it would be cute.

After another half-hour ride through more crowded city streets, the van turned into an alley and stopped outside a big, solid metal gate with sharp points on the top. The missionary pushed a button beside the gate and someone opened it. As they drove inside the mission home compound, Jenny saw three partly cement, partly wooden buildings. She heard the sound of washing machines coming from one of the two-story buildings. A lady carrying a plastic basin of laundry stepped out a door.

Two men stopped shooting baskets and came to help unload their boxes. They opened the van door and Jenny jumped down. She was glad to stretch her legs. She saw children climbing on a jungle gym in the courtyard. A large shorthaired brown dog came up to her and licked her hand. Then a girl got off the monkey bars and ran toward her, asking, "Is your name Jenny?"

"Yes. How did you know?"

"This is going to be your dog," the girl continued. "Her name is—"

"I'm getting a puppy," Jenny started to explain.

"She was ours," the girl went on, not listening. "But we're going on furlough, and we're giving her to your family, you know, aren't we, Mom?" The girl turned toward the lady with the laundry who was now standing by the van. The lady looked over at the big brown dog and began talking to Jenny's mother.

"Do you know what this animal is? I didn't. It's a *carabao* or water buffalo. They help Filipinos with farming and also by pulling carts or as an animal to ride on."

—Jenny

THE PHILIPPINES

Jenny followed her mom up the stairs to their room on the second floor of the mission home. Inside the room, Jenny saw a sink, a desk, a double bed, and a bunk bed. David was already on the lower bunk, because he'd fallen asleep on the way over from McDonald's and Dad had carried him upstairs first thing.

"What's in here?" Jenny asked, opening a door. It was a bathroom and shower, and on the opposite wall from their room was another door. She turned the doorknob. It opened into a room like theirs, except the bedspreads and curtains were different.

"Come back, Jenny," Mom called softly. "Someone else might be staying in that room."

Even though it was the middle of the day, Jenny felt like it was the middle of the night. She climbed the ladder to the top bunk. She wanted to ask about her puppy and about the big brown dog, but she was too tired to think of the words.

When Jenny woke up, it was dark and she heard traffic roaring not far away. A fan hummed as it blew hot air across her sweaty body. A rooster crowed. Lights from outside made lined shadows on the walls. She couldn't think where she was. "Mommy? Daddy?" she called.

"Yes, Dear, are you awake, too?"

Jenny raised herself up and looked down over her bed rail at her parents' bed.

David began to whimper. "Dwink. Dwink."

"That's a good idea," Mom said, as she sat up. "I'll get cold water from the fridge out in the hall." She picked up the pitcher from a tray on the counter by the sink and quietly opened their door.

"Why is it so hot, Daddy?" Jenny asked.

"The Philippines is closer to the equator than where we lived in the States. And Manila is at sea level, and by the ocean, too. It's humid. Shall we turn the air conditioner back on?"

"Yes!" Jenny exclaimed. "I'm so hot I can't breathe. I'm hungry, too," she added, feeling the emptiness in her stomach. But why would she feel so hungry in the middle of the night? And why was she even awake? Why were they all awake?

Dad switched on the desk lamp, reached up and turned on the air conditioner, then went to the windows and pulled them shut. "We bought a few snacks last night just in case," he said, dumping little packages of cookies and chips from a plastic bag onto the bed.

Mom filled the four glasses on the tray by the sink with cold water. Jenny drank every drop and needed more. She began to munch a cookie. "Will we always wake up and eat in the night here in the Philippines?" she asked.

"No," Mom answered. "This is what people call *jet lag*. Remember when Tara's teacher showed you that the Philippine Islands are on the opposite side of the world from the United States? And she told you that

34

it's nighttime here when it's daytime there? Well, our bodies think it's daytime."

"If we were back home now, would it be daytime?" Jenny asked.

"It is daytime there now," her dad answered. "For a few days we'll feel like being awake at night and asleep during the day. But people say it won't be long until our bodies learn the difference. Then we'll be feeling the same as everyone else again."

"I need to write Tara and Connie and Rachel," Jenny said, remembering her promise to her friends.

"You can do that in the morning," her mom said.

Morning? Jenny looked at the clock. Only three-thirty. Here they were, the whole family, awake in the middle of the night, eating snacks and not feeling sleepy. This was kind of fun really, she thought. A dog barked. She remembered the big brown dog. "That big brown dog isn't going to be ours, is it, Mom?"

Her mom and dad looked at each other. "The Smiths are leaving for the United States today," her dad explained, "and need a home for their dog. They'd heard we wanted one and hoped we'd be interested."

"We won't make you keep her," Mom added. "I know you have your heart set on a puppy."

"I do want a puppy, a soft baby puppy." Jenny could almost feel the silky fur of the fat little puppy she imagined to be hers. It would run up to her and wiggle and wiggle until she picked it up. She would hug it gently and it would lick her face. She shivered with excitement.

Just then they all heard a door opening softly, and quiet footsteps in the hall.

"That must be the Smiths getting ready to leave for the airport," Dad guessed. "Since we're all awake, why don't we get dressed and go outside to say good-bye? We won't see them again for a whole year."

When they opened the door to the courtyard, the Smiths were just climbing into the van. Their big brown dog was jumping around and wagging its stumpy tail almost off.

Mrs. Smith spoke quietly, "Lady thinks she's going with us."

After the Smiths and her mom and dad talked a minute, Mr. Smith pulled the van door shut. Lady ran around to the opposite side and put her front feet up on the open window, whining. Then she ran back to the other side. Mr. Smith called out softly, "You'll have to hold her when we drive through the gate."

Dad took hold of Lady's collar. She jumped and pulled. Her whimpering turned into several short barks. "We'll try to find her a good home," Dad said. The van pulled out into the alley, then around the corner toward the street. Mom carefully closed and locked the gate.

Suddenly a squeaking sound surprised them from behind. "Not now, Davy," Dad called quietly; letting go of Lady and turning to catch David who'd found a tricycle. "No one will want to wake up for another couple hours."

They walked toward the mission home door, trying to hush David's protests with whispered promises that he could ride in the morning when the sun came up.

As Dad opened the door, Jenny looked back across the courtyard. A silent shape stood motionless in the shadows, her nose pressed to the bottom of the gate. Then Jenny heard soft whining.

Suddenly Jenny turned and ran toward the gate. She bent down and put both arms around the big dog's neck. She felt Lady's warm body push over against her. "Come on, Lady," she whispered. They walked together to the porch where her family was waiting. "It's all right, Mom and Dad, if Lady is not a puppy," Jenny said, smiling.

A week later, as they loaded a van in the mission home courtyard, Jenny said, "You won't get left behind this time, Lady, I promise."

On the way to the province, where her parents would spend the next year studying the Filipino language, Jenny's dad and the missionary driving them talked quietly together. David soon fell asleep. Mom began to doze.

Jenny watched the huge city of Manila fade into the distant smog behind them. She began to see fields—rice paddies, where people bending over in the hot sun were planting rice plants in straight rows through the water. She saw sugarcane, coconut palms, and broad-leafed banana plants, like in pictures she'd seen in a book from the library back home. Once she saw a man guiding a plow pulled by a lumbering, fat, black animal. "What's that, Dad?" she asked.

Dad looked, but the other missionary answered, "That animal? It's a *carabao,* water buffalo, Jenny."

Jenny also saw dogs and chickens and pigs and, once in a while, another *carabao*. Always there were people. People walking. People talking. Women sweeping dirt yards edged by flowering plants. Little brown children chasing around. Men, women and children sitting on the porches of unpainted wooden houses. Most of the houses had tin roofs, but a few had thatched roofs and woven mat sides. What would their house be like? Would they all sleep together in the same room as they had done at the mission home? How she'd missed Froggie, poor old Froggie! He'd always slept with her. It wasn't fair. She clenched her teeth together and scowled. Why didn't Mom care? Hadn't she said she could take what was special to her? Then she didn't keep her promise.

The van hit another hole in the road. She bounced almost to the ceiling. Mom's head bobbed. Jenny was getting sick and tired of this riding, riding, riding. When would they ever stop? "I need a drink," she called out, not caring that David and her mom were asleep.

"You'll have to wait," her dad answered quietly as he turned to look at her. "When we get there we'll set up the bucket-filter system first thing. We can't drink water from the faucet here like we've been used to," he added.

"No water! No Froggie! No nothing! I—"

"Jenny, that's enough," Dad spoke up sharply.

Mom's head came up. David started to cry.

"We're almost there," said the missionary who was driving. "Do you want to stop at one of these little roadside stores for a Coke? It wouldn't be cold, but it would be wet."

"No. Let's just get there," Mom answered.

Now they were passing house after house on both sides of the road, and churches and stores. More vehicles were on the street. After making several turns, they came to a stop at last. Jenny saw large cement houses. She saw small wooden houses...and one thatch-roofed hut.

A NEW HOME

Jenny couldn't believe it. She ran from room to room over the shiny marble floors, then up the pretty wooden steps to the upstairs. She explored every room. "Mommy, Daddy, come quick," she called. "There's a bedroom for everybody."

The two-story, cement-block house was beyond every imagination. Even Mom said, "I never expected it to be this nice. I like it. I can't wait to get started unpacking." And she started that minute. Dad and the other missionary began working on the water filter set-up.

Suddenly, Jenny remembered her box had been forgotten. She burst into tears.

"What's the matter, Pun'kin?" her dad asked, putting down the large plastic bucket he'd just drilled a hole in. He wrapped his arms around her. Jenny sobbed and sobbed.

Mom stopped digging in a box and came over to her, too. "Jenny, please tell us what's wrong."

"My box... My things..."

"Oh. I'll carry your box up to your room right away if you like," Dad said, working his way through the piles Mom already had out on the floor. He set one box off of another and picked up the bottom one. "Let's go," he said, lifting the heavy cardboard box and starting up the stairs. Jenny felt like singing.

"Are you OK now, Jenny?" Mom asked.

"Yes, I just thought..." She could not tell them what she'd thought. She hurried up the stairs after her dad.

But seeing the box reminded Jenny of those horrid tennis shoes. She would not wear them. Lots of cubbies and cupboards were in the rooms she'd explored. Hiding them would be easy. She would not forgive Mom for bringing them instead of Froggie.

Dad quickly slit the tape on the box with his pocketknife. "There you go," he said, hurrying back downstairs.

Before opening the box, Jenny looked around for a place to stick the tennis shoes until she could find a really good hiding place. Coming back to the box, she spied something green showing though the slit tape. Her eyes widened. She jerked back one of the box flaps and screamed, "Froggie!" Mom had stuffed his head into one tennis shoe and his legs into the other. Jenny grabbed him up and held him tightly against her cheek for a whole minute. He smelled like the new tennis shoes, but she didn't care.

Jenny gently laid Froggie on her bare mattress, giving him an added pat on the head. Then she opened her closet door and placed her new tennis shoes neatly on one of the shelves. She began unpacking. She was almost down to where Charlotte should be when her dad called her for lunch.

"I'm not hungry," she called back.

"Come now," Dad said sternly. He was standing on the landing, holding a very fussy David. "As soon as we eat, I want you to watch Davy, so Mom and I can set up his bed. He's crabby and into everything and needs a nap."

Jenny stomped slowly down the steps. "But I want to finish unpacking," she whined.

"We all have to do our part, Jenny." Mom's voice sounded demanding. The excitement Jenny had seen on her face earlier was gone. The old look she'd had at home during the last few days of packing was back. Jenny decided not to thank her for putting Froggie in her box.

It was one thing after another until the day was gone. The house was the messiest that Jenny had ever seen their home in all her life. The last thing before bed, she had to feed Lady. "Rice?" she exclaimed. "And what's this red stuff?"

"Here in the province," Mom explained, "we make our own dog food. Mrs. Smith said to mix sardines with cooked rice. The sardines are canned in tomato sauce."

"Yuck," Jenny said.

When she woke up the next morning, Lady wasn't barking, but other dogs were. And somewhere puppies were yapping. It seemed to Jenny that she'd heard them all night long. Yap, yap, yap, yap, yap.

And if roosters crowed all night, she'd heard them, too. She went into the hall and opened the window. Looking down into a neighbor's back yard, she counted five roosters. Each was tied to its own stake by a thin rope attached to one leg. Now that the sun was coming up, their crowing never stopped. Jenny had not known before how loud and awful roosters' crowing is.

She heard motorcycles starting up and stopping and starting up again. Somewhere a door slammed. A young child started screaming. Jenny went back into her room and opened her window. Looking out, she saw a wooden house across the street. Next to it, a toddler wearing only an undershirt was splashing in water overflowing from a large round metal basin. The basin was sitting on the ground under a faucet, and a woman squatting by the basin was rinsing clothes.

Just then, two girls came out the open door of the small house. The taller girl was wearing a very white blouse and neat, dark blue skirt, and on her feet were black shoes and white socks. She was carrying a book bag. She walked to the street corner where another girl, dressed exactly the same, was standing. They both got into a motorcycle sidecar and were driven away. Back in the yard, the smaller girl, who was wearing a faded, loose-fitting dress that was slipping off one shoulder, walked toward the woman. She bent down and picked up one of the tightly twisted rolls piling up next to the basin. Shaking it out, she spread it on top of the bushes that lined the edge of their yard.

Jenny closed the window and went downstairs. Mom was holding her little brother on her lap, because they didn't have a high chair for him yet. Jenny thought Davy looked so cute wearing one of his new sunsuits. "Are Filipinos *natives*?" she asked.

"Natives?" Mom asked back without looking at her. "Everyone is a native of somewhere. We are natives of the United States."

"No, you know," Jenny persisted, remembering the girls' question the last time they were together. "Like..." She didn't know what to say exactly. She'd seen missionary slides showing practically naked people running through the jungle with blow guns or squatting by fires, and even sitting in meetings with almost no clothes on.

"Well, the people here in town aren't tribal people, if that's what you mean," Mom said, still giving her attention to feeding David his breakfast. He was giggling and trying to stuff a whole banana into his mouth.

"Go get dressed, Jenny, and I'll fix you some breakfast." Mom glanced her way a second. "The woman who's going to help me here at home will be coming soon."

"What woman?" Jenny asked. Her mother had never had a woman help her at home before.

"I'll explain later. Go get dressed." Without looking Jenny's way again, Mom got up and plopped David on the floor next to a box of his toys. She carried his bowl to the kitchen sink and began talking with Jenny's dad, who was working on something with his tools in the bathroom.

"I hope this woman is dependable with the kids," Jenny heard her mom going on. "Don't know why I'm worried about it. I liked the Filipino women who worked in the dorm that one year I went to the missionary kids' school in Manila."

Jenny slowly climbed the stairs. Strange things were going on. And why wouldn't Mom look at her? Did she know she had planned to tell her the new tennis shoes were lost? Or, was it because she hadn't thanked her for bringing Froggie?

She opened her window a crack to look across the street. The bushes in front of the little house were completely covered with laundry. No one was in the yard now. All she could see were two chickens scratching in the dirt. All she could hear were puppies yapping. She closed the window and started to dress. Then she remembered the new shorts and tops, and Charlotte. She wanted to see her. But what if she was broken? Or what if Mom had taken her out of the box and she hadn't even come at all? Maybe that's why Mom wouldn't look at her.

And why was Lady barking like that all of a sudden?

MOVING IN

After quickly pulling on one of the sets of clothes Mom had laid on her closet shelf, Jenny hurried down the stairs. From the screen door she saw her mom talking with a Filipino woman as they walked together toward the house. David was in Mom's arms and his head was buried in her neck. Lady was still barking.

"Go out and stay with Lady, Jenny, so she'll stop barking," Mom said, as she and the woman stepped inside.

"Where's my breakfast?" Jenny demanded. Her mother frowned at her. Jenny knew the look. She went out, pushing the screen door wide open and letting it go.

Jenny put her arms around her dog's neck, and Lady pushed against her. Lady was trembling, but she'd stopped barking. "It's OK, Lady."

The screen door opened, and Mom helped David outside. "Jenny, play with him for a while out here."

"Where's Dad?" Jenny asked.

"He went into town to the language school to see if someone could help him buy a part for the toilet. Don't let David put anything in his mouth."

"Why do I always have to babysit?" Jenny asked, but her mom was out of sight again. *Anyway, after today,* she thought, *that helper woman will do the babysitting.*

"That woman will take care of you, Davy, you know?" Jenny said. "Mommy and Daddy will go to class every morning, and she'll stay with us."

"No," he responded, bending over and looking closely at a large ant crossing the patio. They followed the ant to the edge of the cement, where it crawled away into a narrow garden lining the inside of the wall surrounding their yard.

"Mommy," David said, heading toward the screen door as Mom and the woman stepped outside. Lady whined but didn't bark.

"These are our children, Jenny and David," Mom said, smiling at Jenny.

"You are cute," the woman said, bending over toward David and pinching his cheek. He let out a cry and clung to Mom.

"He'll be fine as soon as he's used to you," Mom said, picking him up.

You mean he'll be fine as soon as you stop pinching him, Jenny thought.

"How old are you, Jenny?" the woman asked, reaching toward her. Jenny drew back, her cheeks already feeling the sting of a pinch. But the woman only patted her hair and smiled. She had pretty dark brown eyes. She didn't seem nearly as old as Jenny first thought.

"Jenny, can you tell *Ka* Tala how old you are?" Mom prompted.

"Eight."

"*Ka* Tala has four children," Mom said.

"Where are they?" Then, embarrassed by the question popping out of her mouth so fast, Jenny moved close to her mother and looked down at the cement.

When she glanced up, *Ka* Tala was still smiling at her. "My mother-in-law watching two," she answered, "and two going to school already." Then she looked at Jenny's mom and said, "I go now, Ma'am." She opened the gate, went out, reached over the top and latched it again, and left.

"Come inside, kids," Mom said. "I'll fix you a snack before I start unpacking again."

Mom had forgotten she hadn't had breakfast yet. "Is *Ka* Tala coming again tomorrow?" Jenny asked. *Maybe it would be good if she did,* she thought. *At least she would be nice enough to give her breakfast.*

"She'll be back again today," her mom answered. "I've sent her to the market to shop for us. Tonight we'll have a real Filipino meal," Mom explained. She put Davy back on the floor by his toys, then sat a paper bag of little rolls on the table and handed Jenny a banana. "I'm sorry I haven't been listening to you as much as I should lately, Jenny," her mom said as she pulled out a chair and sat down next to her. "Forgive me?"

"Sure, Mom. Thanks for bringing Froggie," she said as she turned and gave her mom a big hug. "I'm sorry for my bad attitudes, Mom."

"I forgive you, too," her mom answered hugging Jenny back. "It's been harder than we thought, hasn't it? Have you finished unpacking your box?"

"Not everything. Is Charlotte in my box, Mommy?"

"If you put her in, she is," Mom answered.

"Do you think she got hurt on the trip?"

"I hope not, but she is very breakable, you know."

"Could Daddy fix her if something broke?"

"I suppose he could try glue."

"Anyway, I have Lady," Jenny said. She decided to go upstairs and unpack Charlotte. Her box was sitting right where she'd left it yesterday. She carefully lifted out the bundle wrapped in the new shorts and tops. Something dropped back into the box.

Jenny caught her breath. *What if...?* She looked down. Oh... just her little wooden music box she'd packed in the folds of Charlotte's dress. She laid the bundle that was Charlotte on her bed and began to open up the layers of clothes. One hand, the other hand, both little feet, her face, she was OK. "Thank you, sweet Charlotte, for not breaking. I love you," Jenny exclaimed. She gently kissed her on one pink cheek. They hadn't been able to bring Charlotte's rocking chair, so Jenny carefully set her by Froggie on her bed.

By the end of the week, her parents had bought more furniture and almost everything was put away. Jenny had a rattan cabinet in her room. The shelf just under the rounded top made a perfect place for Charlotte. The bottom of the cabinet had two shelves inside cupboard doors. Here she'd put her games, art and writing stuff, and a pile of craft kits Grandma had given her to bring. Grandma's music box was in a special place next to Charlotte on the top shelf. On the middle shelf she'd put a few books, her jewelry box, and pictures of her three best friends. Oh, how she ached to see them! Here in the Philippines, she had no one.

By the end of the second week, Jenny was bored. Every day was the same. Get up in the morning. Eat breakfast. Watch *Ka* Tala wash dishes, then clothes. Like the woman across the street, she used big round basins on the ground, but she hung up their laundry with Mom's clothespins on ropes Daddy had put over the patio.

Ka Tala picked up toys and made beds. Jenny used to have to make her own bed, but now she saw that if she didn't make it right when she got up, *Ka* Tala would do it. *Ka* Tala gave them lots more snacks than Mom would, too.

After her parents got home from language school and had eaten lunch, Jenny and her mom did homeschooling while David took a nap. Dad went out to practice his *Tagalog* language in the market or with a man down the street. Mom tried to practice *Tagalog* with *Ka* Tala. Sometimes she said it all wrong, so Jenny would say it.

"Why do you always forget how to say it, Mom?" Jenny asked. Mom didn't answer.

Every day was the same outside, too. Roosters crowed all day and half the night. Puppies yapped. Motorcycle cars drove back and forth, back and forth. Jenny now knew these motorcycles with covered sidecars were called *tricycles* and that they were like taxis. The man across the street was a *tricycle* driver, so they heard his loud motorcycle roaring early before daylight when he left and late after dark when he came home.

Jenny watched the family across the street from her bedroom window. She was glad she didn't always have to carry her little brother around on her hip like the little girl. And she was glad Davy didn't have to just play in the dirt with only sticks for toys. And that Mom always put clothes on him.

More than anything, Jenny wanted to go home. But she didn't have a home in the United States anymore. And this certainly wasn't home. She plain didn't have a home, anywhere. And she missed her friends and Grandma. All she had was Lady. Lady didn't bark now when *Ka* Tala came. She wagged her stumpy tail and acted just as excited to see her as she was to see Mom and Dad when they came home from class.

One morning, when Jenny went downstairs, her dad sat down and took her on his lap. He hadn't done this in a long time. "We have to tell you some sad news, Jenny," he began.

"What?" Her heart began pounding. "What is it?"

"Something happened to Lady last night. She was lying by the gate this morning."

"What do you mean?" Jenny couldn't imagine.

"She wasn't breathing," Dad said.

"She's dead?" Jenny jumped off Dad's lap and went to the screen door. Lady was lying motionless on the cement. Jenny couldn't move. Everything got blurry. She turned and ran into her mom's open arms. "What—what hap-pened?" Mom sat down and took her onto her lap.

"We think someone gave her meat with poison in it," Dad answered.

"Why? But, why?" Jenny wailed.

They were still sitting together when they heard *Ka* Tala open the gate. "Ma'am? Sir?" she began calling loudly.

Jenny got up and ran upstairs. She threw herself on her bed and cried.

She heard *Ka* Tala talking excitedly to Mom and Dad on the patio below her bedroom window. "You know, this is what they do when they planning to rob…" Her voice quieted suddenly, and Jenny couldn't hear the rest of what she was saying.

VISITORS

A few minutes later Jenny heard someone coming up the stairs. *Probably Ka Tala,* she thought. It was past time for her parents to go to class. Why did they always have to go?

"I'm so sorry, sweetie." It was Mom. She sat down on the bed and ran her fingers through Jenny's hair.

Jenny sat up and sobbed in her mom's arms for a long time. "Aren't you late for class, Mom?" she asked finally.

"I'm not going this morning, Dear. I want to stay here with you. I feel sad about Lady, too." Mom's eyes filled with tears.

"May we go back home?" Jenny pleaded. "I mean to our real home. I mean…"

"I know," her mom said soothingly, breathing out a big sigh. She got up and opened the window. "Jenny, come here."

Jenny went to her window. She couldn't believe what she saw. Across the street in the neighbor's yard was her little brother squatting in the dirt and surrounded by yapping puppies. *Ka* Tala stood nearby talking to the woman. The young girl and her little brother giggled as they watched the wiggling puppies licking Davy's face and almost pushing him over.

"Do you want to go out there with Davy, Jenny?"

"No."

"*Ka* Tala told me she is related to that family," Mom continued.

"Why don't you tell her to bring him home?" Jenny snapped. "Anyway, what is going to happen to Lady?"

"Your dad moved her to a shady place by our wall. He'll ask someone from the language school to help him bury her as soon as they get out of class this noon."

Jenny turned from the window and threw herself face down on her bed again. "Somebody's so mean," she sobbed. She pounded the mattress with her fists as hard as she could.

"Let's ask Jesus to help us forgive," her mom said, coming over and taking Jenny's hands in hers and pulling her up into a hug.

"Why did *Ka* Tala say someone might rob us, Mommy?" Jenny asked.

"She told us that people get rid of the family's dog first, so it won't bark and warn anyone when they come back at night."

"Do you think we will get robbed tonight?" Jenny asked, suddenly feeling sick and shaky.

"I hope not," her mom answered. "Let's pray. Would you like to pray first, Jenny?"

"No."

"OK. I'll go ahead. Father," Mom prayed, "please help Jenny and me to forgive. Help us to really love the Filipino people. And please protect us from danger..."

So Mom did think they might get robbed! Jenny reached out and pulled Froggie close to her. She rubbed his worn green furry legs. While her mom prayed, Jenny looked over at beautiful, sweet Charlotte. She loved her so much, even when Lady was still alive. She saw the tiny wooden music box and her few favorite books. She thought about the art supplies and pile of craft kits Grandma had bought especially for her to bring to the mission field. She didn't have nearly a quarter of the things she'd had back home. And now God was going to let somebody take these away, too! Why didn't God care? Jenny felt angry and scared.

"Now I'd like to fix us a special breakfast," Jenny heard her mom saying.

She hadn't realized her mom was finished praying. "Oh, OK," she answered.

"While you make our breakfast, may I go out and see Lady?" Jenny asked.

"Sure, I think that would be OK."

Jenny wanted to see her, and at the same time she didn't want to see her. Out by the wall, she squatted beside her dog. Jenny cried softly as she patted Lady's cold body. "Poor Lady," Jenny sobbed. "You were the only friend I had in all of the Philippines, and now you are dead."

Later that afternoon while working on her school seatwork, Jenny fell asleep. Now she felt a hand on her arm. She lifted up her head from her desk and saw *Ka* Tala standing beside her. "You have visitor, Jenny," she said.

"Me?" Jenny could not imagine a visitor. She didn't know anyone. She got up slowly and peered through the screen door. All she could see over the solid metal gate was the head of a Filipino girl. The girl's dark eyes were looking at her.

"She wants to see me?" Jenny asked again, looking up at *Ka* Tala.

"Yes. I go with you." *Ka* Tala took Jenny by the hand and pulled her gently out the door toward the gate.

Now Jenny saw a smaller girl standing behind the taller one. They were the girls who lived across the street, and the younger one was holding a cute, wiggly puppy.

Ka Tala opened the gate and motioned the girls inside. Moving barely up to the gate, the girl set the puppy down. She smiled shyly up at Jenny then quickly stepped back behind her sister.

The older girl spoke slowly and quietly, "We sorry what happening to your dog."

Jenny looked up at *Ka* Tala.

"They want... They giving you puppy, Jenny," she said, picking it up and holding it out to Jenny. The puppy was squirming and yipping and trying to reach its face toward hers. Its soft blond fur rubbed against Jenny's cheek. She reached out and took the puppy. It wiggled and whined and licked her face.

Jenny looked at the Filipino sisters standing by her gate in their colorful cotton dresses. They smiled at her. How pretty they were with their clean, golden skin; their thick, shiny, black hair; and dark, sparkling eyes!

"Thank you," Jenny said, smiling back at them as she cuddled the warm puppy in her arms.

After supper, Jenny was dishing up rice and sardines for her puppy when she heard her father pounding on the back door with his hammer.

"I didn't know the door was broken, Daddy," she called.

"It's not. I'm just putting on a lock I bought today," he answered. "By the way, a man helped me bury Lady this afternoon while you were napping. Her grave is in a nice place behind our wall."

"May I go see it now, Daddy?"

"Not tonight, Pun'kin. But I'll take you back there tomorrow and you can put flowers on the place if you want to."

Jenny set Lady's food dish on the floor for her puppy. The dish went slipping and sliding all over the shiny, waxed floor, as the puppy tried to eat as fast as she could. Jenny giggled. She walked into the back room where her father was putting away his tools. "Do I have to let my new puppy sleep outside like Lady did?"

"She is pretty little," her father answered, "but she's not used to staying inside. I'll tie her close to the door, so she'll be safe."

Jenny noticed two locks on the door besides the new one. "Why did you put another lock on our door, Dad?" she asked

"Oh, people do that here in the Philippines, Jenny."

"Are we going to be robbed tonight, Daddy?"

"I hope not, Pun'kin."

"Daddy, can we pray right now and ask God to keep us safe?"

"Sure. Do you want to pray, or do you want me to?"

"Let's both pray because I want to ask God to bless those Filipino girls who gave me my new puppy." And before she prayed out loud, Jenny quietly asked God to help her to forgive.

After she was tucked into bed that evening, Jenny heard her parents going around locking all of the windows in their house, even the ones upstairs.

ANGEL

———— ⌘ ————

Every night they locked everything, but no one ever came. Every morning Jenny's family thanked God for protecting them. The day after they buried Lady, *Ka* Tala brought a bunch of flowers and had gone with Jenny to put them on her grave. Even though *Ka* Tala was an adult, she and Jenny were becoming good friends.

One day, while Jenny watched *Ka* Tala scrub clothes in a large basin of soapy water on the patio by their back door, Jenny asked, "Do you think my new little puppy scared the robbers away?"

"Yes. Your puppy good watchdog," *Ka* Tala answered. "My sister-in-law tell me her brother hearing one *trike* driver. He say man tell him somebody trying a robbery at house that belong to Doctora Mendosa. Her neighbor shoot at them. They don't think they trying anymore to rob somebody still."

"Good." Jenny sighed with relief.

Ka Tala continued, "The brother of my sister-in-law is father of Angel. Angel the one giving you puppy. She tell her father she like being friend to you."

"How old is Angel?"

"Eight already. Same like you."

"Eight?" Jenny asked. "Why doesn't she go to school like her sister?"

"Because they not able to support her school need right now. The uniform. The book. The cost too high. She know how to read, 'cuz she graduate already grade two. She tell her father she really want book to read."

Jenny looked through a small space between their side yard gate and the high wall. Angel was gathering laundry off the bushes and carrying it into her house. She could use only one arm, because her other arm was holding her small brother on her hip.

Jenny handed clothes to *Ka* Tala as she pinned them on the line. Next, *Ka* Tala started cleaning rice. She put it in a round, flat basket. She jerked the basket with her hands, flipping the rice up in the air. Pieces of stuff blew away. Now and then, she stopped to pick out a tiny, black rock. Jenny saw through the space that Angel's mother was cleaning rice, too.

That afternoon, when Jenny and her mom finished their homeschooling, Jenny asked, "Mom, could I give Angel a present?"

"Is that the little girl who gave you the puppy? That would be nice, Dear. What do you think she might like?"

"I know what she wants," Jenny answered right away.

Her mom looked surprised. "You do?" she asked.

"Yes. She wants a book to read."

"But Jenny, what makes you think she knows how to read? I've never seen her going to school."

"I know," said Jenny, "but *Ka* Tala says she used to. She's finished second grade. Now her family can't afford it. Mom, could we give them money, so she can go back to school?"

"Daddy and I can talk about it, Dear."

When *Ka* Tala arrived the next morning, Jenny showed her a pretty wrapped package. Angel's name was written on a small hand-decorated card taped on the top. "Will you take this to Angel?" she asked.

"I go with and you take," suggested *Ka* Tala.

Jenny hesitated. "I don't know…"

"Most probably, Angel be happy you coming." *Ka* Tala took the package in one hand and picked up Davy in her other arm. She led Jenny out the gate and across the street. Jenny felt excited and nervous.

Instead of going into the part of the yard Jenny could see from her house, *Ka* Tala led her around to the other side. In front of the house close to the street was an open-front shack. Behind a low counter, Jenny saw a shelf holding bottles of cloudy white liquid and bottles of different shades of brown liquid. She also saw one can of sweetened condensed milk, one can of fruit cocktail, and several cans of sardines. On another shelf, she saw different kinds of snacks and a big glass jar half full of the cough-drop things she had tasted her first day in the Philippines. On the ground was a case of Pepsi bottles, some full and some empty.

"Does this store belong to Angel's family?" whispered Jenny.

"Yes. Her *nanay*—her grandmother—owner of this s*ari-sari* store."

In a minute, an old woman came slowly from the house. Angel came, too, half hidden behind her grandmother's long, brown dress. Jenny and Angel smiled shyly at one another. Angel's eyes kept turning toward the package in *Ka* Tala's hand. *Ka* Tala talked with the old woman in *Tagalog*. *Nanay* rubbed her wrinkled hand over Davy's arms, but she didn't pinch him.

Pretty soon *Nanay* turned and took two bags of chippies from the shelf, then dumped a few pieces of sticky, red candy into a plastic bag. *Ka* Tala set Jenny's package on the counter, took several coins from her pocket, and put them into *Nanay's* hand. Angel kept smiling at Jenny, but neither she nor the old woman touched the present.

Ka Tala picked up the snacks, and they walked back across the street. Once inside her house, Jenny asked, "Why didn't Angel pick up my present and open it?"

"Oh, she not doing that when you right there, Jenny!"

All morning Jenny had been imagining how Angel might look when she opened her present and saw the book she and her mother had wrapped for her. She felt so disappointed.

"But why wouldn't she open it?" Jenny asked again.

"She… We Filipino…" *Ka* Tala continued mostly in *Tagalog*, and Jenny could not understand. *Maybe Angel didn't really want to be friends*, Jenny thought. She felt very sad.

Two days later, *Ka* Tala said, "Tomorrow afternoon I stop working and go to birthday party. The baby brother of Angel will already be two-year-old tomorrow. Angel asking me, 'Jenny will come, too?' I say, 'yes.' I hoping you allowed. By the way," she added, "you can bring *Totoy* little gift."

TOTOY'S BIRTHDAY PARTY AND ALL SAINTS' DAY

"I don't like the way she takes off work all the time to visit the neighbor," Jenny heard her mom saying the next morning when she woke up. "And I don't know what she's giving David to eat all morning, but lately he hardly touches his lunch."

"You'd better sit down and talk to Tala," Jenny's father said. "Tell her you will hold back some of her pay if she keeps doing what you ask her not to."

"I'd much rather do my housework myself. It's not all getting done anyway. And, do you know she sometimes talks to the children in *Tagalog*, and I don't even know what she says to them?"

Then Jenny heard her mother blowing her nose.

Even though it didn't seem like a good time to mention it, as soon as she was downstairs, Jenny said, "Don't forget to buy a gift for me to take to *Totoy*'s birthday party."

Her mother just responded with a big sigh.

The birthday party was not at all what Jenny expected. She wasn't surprised when her gift for *Totoy* was added to a pile on the table and not touched again during the party. But she was surprised when the beautifully decorated birthday cake beside the gifts went untouched, too!

The book she had given to Angel was lying on the coffee table. Angel, who was wearing another pretty cotton dress, sat down on a stiff straight chair next to Jenny. She laid her small brown hand on Jenny's arm and smiled at her.

"Your dress is pretty," Jenny said.

"My mother make. It old already," Angel said, "but yours really pretty."

Her own dress was regular, Jenny thought, but Angel's dress looked quite new.

Totoy, on the other hand, dressed in a cute sailor outfit, seemed proud of how he looked. Jenny wondered if he felt uncomfortable wearing all those clothes. He was showing off terribly, while the many adults in the crowded room smiled and smiled as they watched his on-going antics. In his slippery-bottomed shoes, *Totoy* kept wiping out on the highly waxed gray cement floor. Everybody laughed. Jenny couldn't help but think of the different kind of attention her own two-year-old brother would get had he acted like that.

Ladies were bringing in food and putting it on a table set up in one end of the room. Jenny noticed that the room where the food was being prepared had a dirt floor. The only other room in the house was behind a curtained doorway.

"We sleeping in that room," Angel said. Jenny felt embarrassed. Angel must have been watching her stare all around her house.

"How many are in your family, Angel?" she asked.

"*Inay* and *Tatay*—Mama and Papa. *Totoy*, me, *Ate* Ana—my older sister—and *Kuya* Jun—my eldest brother—but he not always sleeping with us. Oh, and *Nanay*. *Nanay* like better sleeping on floor in *sala* (*sah-lah*)—this room. She say it cooler. And, I think," Angel added hesitantly, "we have our two more brother but they not live here to our place."

"What?" Jenny could not think what she meant. Angel didn't know if she had two more brothers or not?

"I not know for sure," Angel finished, leaving Jenny puzzled.

Somebody finally took *Totoy* somewhere. Other small children disappeared, too. The adults were sitting wherever they could, everyone talking at the same time. Most of the men went outside where they began drinking something. Jenny turned to Angel and asked, "Can you come to my house and play with me tomorrow?"

"Yes. Maybe. It depend. We preparing for tomorrow night. Will you go to cemetery?"

"Why?" Jenny asked, puzzled by this question.

"Our grandfather there. Our family staying all night with him."

"What does he do at the cemetery?" Jenny asked.

Now Angel looked puzzled. She did not seem to know how to answer Jenny. After a minute, she said, "We take lot of foods. We singing and playing game. People telling joke. Every person's family going."

"To the cemetery? At night?" Jenny asked. She couldn't think why they'd want to do that.

"All night and next day. It All Saints' Day. Do you have All Saints' Day in the States?" Angel asked.

"I don't know," Jenny answered, feeling confused.

Angel took her hand. "I come to your place tomorrow," she said, smiling. "Now we eat our *pansit* we make."

The ladies filled Jenny's plate with the tasty noodle dish they had made.

After they ate, Angel said, "I will walk to your gate." Hand in hand, they crossed the street.

As Angel turned to leave, Jenny waved and called, "See you tomorrow." Angel smiled.

But Angel did not come the next day. In fact, *Ka* Tala didn't come either. A girl they didn't know came to their gate with a note from *Ka* Tala. "Sorry, Ma'am," it said, "I will come day after tomorrow again."

So Jenny's mom got to stay home and do her own work. But it didn't seem to be making her very happy, Jenny thought. Jenny played with her puppy on the patio. Puppy was learning to fetch. Whenever the little dog came to a fast stop, after running to pick up whatever Jenny threw, she wiped out on the smooth cement. Jenny giggled and giggled.

Then she heard her mother calling down to the patio from the window above. "You didn't make your bed, Jenny, and your room is a mess."

"Oh, oh," Jenny said quietly to Puppy. She remembered how she always had to clean up her room back in the States. Now she was so used to letting *Ka* Tala do it, she sometimes forgot about it on the days she didn't come to work. She left the puppy chewing on a pork bone and trudged inside, over a pile of dirty laundry, and up the stairs.

"Do you let *Ka* Tala do this for you when I'm gone, Jenny?" her mother asked.

"Maybe sometimes."

"Well, you are to do it yourself every day, Young Lady," her mother announced. "You are not to ask *Ka* Tala to do your work for you."

"You do," Jenny retorted, getting into the same bad mood her mother seemed to be in.

"You can stay right here in your room until your father comes home," her mom responded. She scooped up David, who had just dumped Jenny's markers all over the floor, and went downstairs.

Jenny lay on her unmade bed in her messy room and read a book the rest of the morning. Just before noon, she jumped up and put everything away and made her bed. When her father came in, her room was neat.

"Sorry, Daddy," Jenny said right away.

"You'd better go down and say that to your mother," her father ordered.

The next day was a holiday in the Philippines, so Jenny and her family spent a special happy day together, taking time for projects, games and stories. Her parents had learned about All Saints' Day in their culture class. "It's something like Memorial Day in the States," Jenny's dad said. He explained to Jenny that people in the Philippines visit the cemetery where their dead relatives are buried, often staying the night before.

"Oh," Jenny said, "no wonder Angel didn't know what to say when I asked what her grandfather did at the cemetery!"

The next afternoon, Angel came over, so Jenny's mom let her stop her homeschooling lessons early. Angel told them she'd never been in an American house before. "But aren't you so lonely sleeping to yourself?" she asked when she saw Jenny's bedroom. Her face looked so sad.

"No, I've always had my own room," Jenny explained. "Do you really like to sleep in the same room with all your family?"

"Oh, yes. We sleeping together under family-size mosquito net."

Angel openly stared all around Jenny's room. Jenny was a little surprised when she went around opening every door and drawer and picking up each thing on her shelf. But actually, it was really fun for Jenny to watch Angel looking at and feeling so many things she had never touched before.

Later in the afternoon, Jenny's mom called the girls downstairs for a tea-party *merienda* she'd fixed for them. Angel seemed very happy, but not happier than Jenny, who had really missed not having a human friend her own age. She was also very pleased that her mother had been so nice to them even though she was having a hard day. Reaching over and giving her mom a big kiss on her cheek, she said, "Thank you for the tea party, Mom."

"My *inay*—my mama—leaving in only two more day already," Angel announced.

"What do you mean, Dear?" Jenny's mom asked.

"She going abroad…to Saudi. She taking sewing job to important man."

"For how long?" Jenny asked, not believing her ears.

"One year only. She coming home next All Saints' Day."

"But you have a little brother only two years old," Mom said, looking very concerned. "Who will take care of him, and you?"

"Our *nanay*."

Jenny remembered the old woman at the s*ari-sari* store. She could hardly walk.

"Aren't you sad?" Jenny asked.

"It OK. It help support our family need."

"Don't you care if she's gone for a whole year?" Jenny asked, not believing what she'd heard.

"I will miss her, yes, of course," Angel answered, the corners of her mouth turning down. Then smiling, she added, "But our family helping each other get along." After pausing a second, she turned to Jenny, "*Inay* say I invite you ride to Manila when we going to airport. We hire *jeepney*."

After Angel left, Jenny asked, "How could Angel say it was OK? Her mother shouldn't leave and go far away to another country for a whole year. What will poor *Totoy* do?" Jenny thought about her own little brother. He could never get along without his mother. And really, neither could she. Jenny felt sad and angry.

"I remember," her mom said as she stood by the door looking across the street, "when I was at the MK school in Manila, one of the maids who worked there had a toddler and a baby at home. Because she lived too far away to travel every day, she was only able to see them from Saturday afternoon 'till Sunday afternoon. I felt so sorry for her and her little children. Sometimes I got up and did her early Monday morning work before school so she could stay at home one more night."

Only half listening, Jenny was thinking about Angel's invitation. A trip to Manila on a *jeepney*! "May I go?" She looked at her mother pleadingly.

"Go where?"

"To Manila on a *jeepney* with Angel's family."

Mom didn't answer. Jenny knew she'd never be allowed to go.

"You should see some of the *jeepneys* in Manila! They have lots of horses and mirrors on the hood and other decorations, too, especially on the front window. Many have pictures painted on the sides. Some are plain. All have a sign telling where they are going. I ride in *jeepneys* when we go on longer trips and when we are in Manila. We also ride in buses and taxis."

—Jenny

JEEPNEY RIDE

"May I puleeeez go?" Jenny begged the next night at supper for the fiftieth time that day. Candlelight flickered on her pleading face, as she slurped the potato soup her mom had made.

"Stop slurping," her mother responded. "I hope the electricity comes back on soon. I can't stand this much longer, tonight!"

Jenny knew it was really hard on her mom whenever the electricity went off. And these brownouts always happened when it was dark or hot or stormy, just when it was needed the most. But her mom was putting off answering her question. She'd never said she definitely couldn't go.

"Mom? Dad?"

"I go jeep?" Davy added, squinting his small face into a pitiful expression.

"Oh, my," Mom sighed. She whipped the woven hand fan back and forth in front of her, causing the candle flame to wave violently and sending black smoke trailing toward the ceiling.

"I guess you can go. Your father thinks you'll be OK."

Jenny jumped up to give her mom a hug, upsetting her chair, which went crashing over on the marble tile floor. David, caught up in the excitement of the victory, blew a big puff of air toward the table, putting out the candle. Pitch darkness took over.

"Everybody stay right where you are," Jenny's father spoke, as his chair could be heard scraping against the floor. "Where are the matches?"

But just then the electricity came back on. The fluorescent ceiling light's flickering on and the fan's welcome breeze improved everyone's mood immediately. Jenny started right in clearing the table.

"She will be fine, Ma'am," *Ka* Tala told Jenny's mom the next morning as she stepped out the door with Jenny.

When *Ka* Tala asked to be off work so she could go, too, Jenny's mom had said she didn't like to miss another day of classes, but she guessed she'd feel better knowing *Ka* Tala was along with Jenny. "Come to the house as soon as you get back, Tala," Mom called after them. "There's a lot of work piling up here."

Mom's voice faded into the background, as Jenny approached the bustling commotion around the house across the street. Angel ran out the open door and grabbed her hand. Angel was excited enough, but *Totoy* was totally wild. He chased a yapping, black puppy in and out the door, fighting to stay on his feet every time he hit the slippery, waxed floor inside. Then boy and dog sprawled over a pile of suitcases and bags. Everyone laughed. *Totoy* howled, but was quickly pacified by candy stuffed into his mouth by one of the adults.

"Soon *Tiyo* Romy—Uncle—bringing *jeepney*," Angel told Jenny.

Jenny looked at the crowd of people milling around inside and outside. "Who all is going on the *jeepney*?" she asked Angel.

"All our family—*Tatay*, and of course, *Inay*, and *Totoy*, *Ate*, *Nanay*; and *Tiya* Nene, sister of our mother. And *Kuya*—you not meet our eldest brother yet—and of course, *Ate* Tala, and I don't know who more," she ended, out of breath.

"Is *Ka* Tala your sister?" Jenny asked surprised.

"No, she only sister-in-law to my... I not know for sure."

Ate Ana and *Nanay* were busy packing *lansones* fruit and little packages of chippies in a plastic bag to take along. Angel's mother was kept busy talking to all the visitors who came to say good-bye, each bringing a small gift of something for her to take abroad with her.

"She will have lot of present to bring back when she come home," Angel remarked.

"What?" Jenny asked.

"She bring something to everybody who giving her gift."

Tiya Nene tried to stuff each new thing into one or another of the suitcases. Finally, she began filling a plastic bag. "Your *inay* have so many friend, Baby," she commented to Angel, patting her cheeks.

"Did she call you 'Baby'?" Jenny whispered.

"Sometime my family calling me that. 'Cuz I'm youngest sister."

Coming back from one of her trips to the door, Angel's mother noticed Jenny. "Oh, it good thing you come with us. I like you being friend to Angel. You look like American girl I know in Manila, only she high schooler. She very kind to me. Sometimes she help me so I'm able staying home longer with my Jun and baby Ana. Many year ago when I work to missionary kids' school. Jun already going on eighteen and Ana going on sixteen.

Just then a young man, smoking a cigarette, strolled in the door.

"*Hoy*, Jun," called Angel's father as he came through the curtained bedroom door. "Do you know our Baby got now American friend?" he said, pointing his lower lip in Jenny's direction.

"Hello," Jun said, nodding his head slightly and smiling at her.

"This my *kuya*," Angel whispered proudly in Jenny's ear.

Before Jenny could respond, she heard a roaring motor and honking. The *jeepney* had arrived. Angel took Jenny's hand and pulled her through the doorway. A man jumped out the open space by the front seat.

"*Tiyo* Romy," Angel informed Jenny, "brother of our mother."

"Who are the other three men?" Jenny asked.

Angel looked. "One driver. I think others most probably friend of driver."

Angel's father and brother began loading bags onto the floor in the back of the *jeepney*, pushing them forward until they were against the back of the front seat. Then everyone piled onto the long side seats, their backs to the open windows behind them.

Nanay struggled to climb up the high step into the back of the *jeepney*. She handed her plastic bag to someone and grabbed the poles on either side of the steps. She pulled while *Tiyo* Romy pushed. As soon as she was seated, she lifted *Totoy* up onto her lap. They all squished together, some almost not on the seat at all. "Are all these people your relatives?" Jenny quietly asked Angel.

"Not all. Some say they only need ride to Manila today."

Tiyo Romy climbed over the spare tire onto the edge of the driver's side of the front seat. The driver reached across *Tiyo* with his left hand and steered the vehicle onto the small side street, in through town, then out onto the highway.

Racing along with other *jeepneys* and busses and cars, her hair blowing all over her face, Jenny could not think of anything more fun. She squirmed to turn and look out the window behind her. They were flying past wide-leafed banana plants, flowering trees, tall coconut palms, sugarcane fields, and rice paddies.

Everyone laughed and joked.

Each barrio they passed seemed like all the others. The highway became the main street, lined with small open-front businesses. Mini marts, pharmacies, hardware stores with metal stuff stuck everywhere, clothing stores with T-shirts hanging from the ceilings, and eateries with stool-lined counters filled with heavy, aluminum rice pots and a big, glass jug of yellow drink. Slow-moving *tricycles* driving ahead of them, double-parked trucks, *jeepneys* pulling out or backing up, people walking, people sitting, people everywhere.

Jenny saw long, low buildings where uniformed school children played at recess or stood in line ready to go inside. She noticed churches, especially the beautifully clean, neatly painted ones with spires and steeples, called *Iglesia ni Cristo*.

Each time they slowed down in busy traffic, vendors held trays of food up to the windows by the children. Angel looked at her *kuya*. He shrugged his shoulders and held up open hands, as if to say he had no money. *Totoy* began to throw a fit. The driver turned around and looked back over his shoulder. *Nanay* looked at *Kuya* Jun. He slid forward and reached down into his pocket, then turned toward the window behind him.

"Four *espesol* and eight Coke," he told a vendor. He passed the plastic bags of pop inside. Four went to the front seat, and the people in back shared the other four. The *espesol*—sweet, sticky-rice rolled in powdered sugar—was given to the children, but of course they allowed little bites to the adults, who in turn let the children sip Coke through straws inserted into the plastic bags. Chippies were shared around, and small firm white *lansones* sections were squeezed out of their peeling into ready mouths.

After *merienda*, the children fell asleep on shoulders and laps while the adults quietly dozed.

When Jenny awoke, they were slowing down. Vehicles filled the expressway. Traffic inched along. Air-conditioned busses towered above them. Continuing on into the city, she began to see yellow taxis weaving in and out, taking any small, available, open space. Noise and exhaust fumes filled the air. The women held white, folded handkerchiefs over their noses and mouths. *Nanay* continued to doze.

Then their *jeepney* swung into a turn and slowly moved along in a line of cars and taxis and *jeepneys* toward a long building. At first, Jenny didn't recognize the airport where she had arrived in the Philippines just a few months ago. Uniformed men were loading all kinds and sizes of boxes and bags and suitcases from the sidewalk onto carts and wheeling them through big glass doors into the building. Now Jenny remembered.

The *jeepney* stopped by the sidewalk. Angel and *Totoy*, and even *Ate* Ana had never seen an airport before. *Kuya* Jun called *Totoy*, Angel and Jenny to look up at a roaring jet coming in low overhead. They stuck their heads out the window. The whole *jeepney* vibrated. "Wow! Wow!" *Totoy* screamed, hanging far out the window as *Kuya* Jun held him by the back of his pants. The jet soared beyond their view.

The children pulled their heads inside and turned around. The back of the *jeepney* was empty, except for *Nanay*. The people were gone. The luggage was gone. *Inay* was gone! Angel burst into tears. She moved close against her grandmother who slipped her old, wrinkled, brown arm around her.

As Jenny watched, not knowing what to do or think, *Totoy* suddenly seemed to realize his mother was gone. "*Inay, Inay*," he cried. He pulled away from *Kuya* Jun and fell down on the *jeepney* floor, kicking. He threw his head back and forth. "*Inay! Inay!*" he screamed.

Kuya Jun pulled a small plastic airplane from his pocket. "If you stop, you can have airplane," he yelled to *Totoy* over the crying. *Totoy* grabbed for the airplane, but *Kuya* Jun pulled it back. "Stop crying," he yelled again. Now *Totoy* was standing up. *Kuya* Jun kept the toy out of his reach. Finally, *Totoy* stopped and he let him have the airplane.

Jenny looked back at Angel, who was still quietly sobbing into a handkerchief. *She does care a lot,* Jenny thought. Poor Angel. Poor *Totoy*. Poor family. *How can I help them?* she wondered.

ATE ANA

The *jeepney* trip from Manila back to the province that hot afternoon was a quiet one. Because it had started to rain, the plastic fastened above the window openings behind the seats had been unrolled. It wasn't possible to see out except through places in the windshield that weren't covered with stickers. After stopping at an eatery for rice and *ulam*—meat-flavored vegetables in broth—almost everyone slept. Jenny fell sound asleep with her head on *Ate* Ana's lap.

When she awoke, *Ate* Ana was stroking her sweaty hair. "Almost to our place, Jenny," she said. *Ate* Ana wiped her face. Jenny was surprised to see big black smudges appearing on the clean white handkerchief. She wondered how she could have slept the whole trip home, but she must have. Just ahead, she saw her mother standing under an umbrella by their gate.

The *jeepney* came to a stop. "Good-bye, good-bye," different ones called, as Jenny jumped off the high, back step of the *jeepney* and scooted under her mother's umbrella. Jenny turned and waved as the *jeepney* pulled away.

"You look filthy. Look at your arms! Have you had a drink? I hope you didn't drink something made from unboiled water," Jenny's mother kept going on. "I didn't think the trip would take all day. What was I thinking, letting you go by yourself? Are you alright?"

"Yes, Mom, I—"

But her mom was still talking. "As soon as you have a drink, go right upstairs and take a bath. Where's *Ka* Tala?"

"I don't know. She came back with us. Maybe she got off when I was sleeping."

"So another day gone and the ironing not done again," Mom sighed. "I don't know what I'm going to do!"

"I had fun," Jenny began.

"Please. Go get your bath, Jenny. You can tell us about it this evening. Right now I have to study for the language test tomorrow and then start supper."

"Where's David, Mom?"

"He's still sleeping. I didn't get him down for his nap until late. Now I suppose he'll be up until ten o'clock tonight. Hurry, Jenny, so you can watch him for me when he wakes up."

"Mom—"

"Not now." Jenny's mother sat down at the table, opened her language book, switched on the tape recorder, and began repeating phrases.

Jenny didn't try asking her to heat water for her bath. The cold water she dumped over herself from the bucket in the shower stall didn't feel too terrible after such a hot, sticky trip. It felt good to wash her hair and scrub the black soot off her body.

"I hope the electricity doesn't go off tonight," Jenny's mother said, as they sat down to supper an hour later than usual. "I can't stand one more thing today, or I'll lose my mind—what's left of it!"

"Mom," Jenny ventured carefully. "*Ate* Ana could come to work for us after she gets home from school in the afternoons. She could do the ironing and you could have more time to study. Her mother used to work for missionaries in Manila when *Ate* Ana was a baby." At least she'd gotten that far without anyone interrupting. Her mother didn't say anything, so Jenny continued, "Their family needs money really bad. I know *Ka* Tala said it would embarrass them if we just gave them money, but *Ate* Ana could help you do your work, and you could pay her."

"Who is *Ate* Ana, Jenny?" her mother asked.

"Angel's sister—the one who helped her bring over our puppy."

"How old is she?" her father asked. "She looked awfully young to take a job."

"She's almost sixteen, Dad. Angel said she will graduate from high school in March."

"Filipino schools do only have ten grades," her father commented.

"*Ate* Ana said she wants to start college next summer," Jenny added, "but there's no money now. And Angel really wants to go to school. If *Ate* Ana could work, maybe Angel could go back to school. Please, Mom?"

"Oh, my," Mom sighed, putting her head in her hands. "I don't like to think of having two helpers around here. I feel so overwhelmed now, but..."

"I think we should try it," Dad said firmly. "You can't keep going like you have lately."

Then Jenny saw something she had never seen before. Her mother started sobbing. Jenny was horrified. She didn't know grown-ups ever did that. She didn't know what to do.

So that is how it happened that *Ate* Ana started coming to work every afternoon at four o'clock. She watched David and played with Jenny. She helped Mom prepare supper. After supper she washed dishes, and before leaving, she ironed everything *Ka* Tala had not been able to finish earlier.

Jenny's mom began to look more relaxed. At least half of her studying was finished by suppertime. She could take time to sit down with the family when they read together after supper. And Jenny was especially happy when Angel told her that her *Ate* planned to buy her uniform and books, so she would be going to school again when the new term started.

But that night, when Jenny discovered her little music box from Grandma was missing from the shelf where she always kept it, her mother said, "Why don't you ask Ana about it?"

"Mom, *Ate* Ana wouldn't—"

"Jenny, just ask if she has seen it."

RAIN, RAIN, RAIN

It had been raining every day, so clothes could not be dried outside. The whirring noise of several fans set to blow on the wet clothes never stopped. Everything was crowded. Jenny ducked around half-dry laundry hanging on lines in the upstairs hall and bedrooms. Determined to search everywhere until she found her missing music box, she tried to think. Just then *Ka* Tala came up the stairs with a pile of stiff folded clothes, washed three days ago and finally dry.

"When will it ever stop raining?" Jenny asked her.

"It because typhoon passing. It always raining like this. But soon it stop."

"Are we having a typhoon?"

"Rain only. If typhoon hitting us, it make strong wind. It blow over many thing. Sometime blow roof off."

Just then the fans stopped. The clothes quit flapping. Everything became very still.

"Electricity go off," *Ka* Tala said, slipping between two wet towels and into Jenny's bedroom.

Starting to feel scared, Jenny hurried after *Ka* Tala. "Will the typhoon hit us?"

"No, it already pass. It not hit land until far up north."

Jenny decided she could put up with the clutter and musty smell of wet clothes, as long as no typhoon came near them.

Patting Charlotte's curls and gently touching her pink lips with the tip of her finger, *Ka* Tala said, "You have so pretty doll, Jenny. My little girl, they say they wanting doll. But I not find any doll in market, except the cost too high."

Jenny looked sadly at the empty place beside her doll. "*Ka* Tala, did you see my music box anywhere? I always keep it on this shelf, but now it's not here."

A very worried expression came over *Ka* Tala's face. "I not see. It little wood box?"

"Yes. My grandma gave it to me to bring over to the Philippines. It's so special to me. *Ate* wouldn't take it, would she *Ka* Tala?" Now that *Ate* Ana came every day, Jenny just called her *Ate* like Angel did.

"I don't think she take. But asking not good thing, Jenny. If she know you asking, she never work to our place anymore."

"Oh, please, please don't tell her I asked you, *Ka* Tala. I didn't think she would take it. Will you look everywhere for it when you are cleaning?"

"Yes. If I find, I tell to you right away. These girls, friends to you from States?" *Ka* Tala asked, pointing to the pictures of Tara, Connie and Rachel.

"Yes, I miss them so much," Jenny answered. How she longed to see them, even if for only one afternoon! She thought about their last picnic together, the day before she'd left. Did the girls ever think about her anymore?

The following day the rain finally stopped. Jenny's mom had *Ka* Tala rewash everything that smelled bad. A strong wind blew the clothes dry quickly, so even the towels were almost soft for once. The sunshine brightened everyone's mood. And that night while putting on sweet-smelling sleepers, Jenny spied her music box in its place on the shelf. Happily she wound the key on the bottom and listened to the tinkling melody. She thought of what her grandma had said, "Whenever you wind it up and listen to the song, you'll remember I love you." How she ached for a hug from Grandma!

"Oh, you found your music box!" Mom said, coming in to pray with Jenny.

"I don't know who found it. It was just here again on my shelf," Jenny said thankfully.

"Well, that's kind of a mystery, isn't it?" Jenny's mom commented. They knelt together to pray, then Jenny climbed between her freshly washed and dried sheets and fell asleep with Froggie under her arm.

But the next morning, when Dad turned on the radio, they heard, "This powerful typhoon, packing 200 kilometer winds, will make landfall in the Bicol region tomorrow morning and is expected to move north across Luzon…"

Jenny's heart began to thump. "Is this one coming toward us, Daddy?"

"Sounds like it. We'll have to listen to the radio often and keep an ear open. It will be a few days yet."

The day was sunny and beautiful. White, puffy clouds drifted across the blue sky. Jenny's mom must have asked *Ka* Tala to wash every single thing they owned, Jenny observed, as she watched the curtains on the clothesline gently flapping in the breeze. Across the street, clothes were covering the bushes. Someone at Angel's house was washing lots, too.

Ka Tala usually did all the shopping early in the morning on her way to their house. But now Jenny's mother was asking her to go to the market again this afternoon. Jenny begged to go, too. She didn't used to like going to the market, because ladies always came close to stroke her hair and rub their brown fingers over her arms. Sometimes they'd touch her nose or pinch her cheeks. But now she was getting used to it—not the pinching—but she could understand more of what they said to her. Whenever she answered them in *Tagalog*, they made exclamations to each other and acted so pleased.

Today, lots of people were in the market. It seemed that suddenly everyone was buying extra things. Whenever Jenny went along to the market, *Ka* Tala always held her hand, or if not, she had her hold one side of the shopping bag they carried between them.

They passed the banana stall. "*Saging*?" (*sah*-ging) the vendor called out to them. But they hurried on until they saw a seller who still had big yellow mangoes on her table. *Ka* Tala handed the plastic bag of mangoes she'd bought to Jenny to carry. Passing by several tables of different kinds of greens, they stopped and bought green beans and carrots and potatoes.

Then they crossed the street to the mini mart. After giving their bags to a man behind a counter and tucking the ticket he handed her into her pocket, *Ka* Tala put one of the handles of a shopping basket into Jenny's hand. The store was even more crowded than usual, and they had to almost push their way through the aisles with their heavy basket. They collected all the canned things on the list.

Standing on the steps outside after paying for their groceries and exchanging their ticket for their fresh things, *Ka* Tala looked toward the place where *tricycles* parked. "Getting ride home will be hard for us. I see no empty *trike*," she said, frowning. After a few minutes, while bending over to rest their heavy bags on the sidewalk, a *tricycle* stopped by them.

"*Hoy*, Tala," the driver called. Jenny looked up. It was Angel's father.

"Jo Jo, *pala!* (pah-*lah*)" exclaimed *Ka* Tala, looking surprised and relieved. A man already seated inside got out and climbed on the motorcycle seat behind Angel's father. "So many shoppers still!" *Ka* Tala exclaimed to JoJo, as she and Jenny climbed inside the covered sidecar and put their bags on the floor around their feet.

Leaning down to speak to them, Angel's father asked, "Did you hear about typhoon? They say will be direct hit." Then the noise of the motor and booming beat on the radio drowned out their fast *Tagalog* conversation. Jenny could think of nothing except, *Direct hit. Direct hit.* The words echoed in her ears to the beat she heard on the speaker all the way home.

The next day the sun shined all morning, but at noon the sky began filling with clouds. "The clouds are going from north to south. The typhoon is working its way north," Jenny's dad said.

"Has it already passed us, Daddy?" Jenny asked, remembering *Ka* Tala talking about typhoons hitting far up north.

"No. It's still south of us."

"What is a direct hit, Daddy?" Jenny thought she might already have a good idea of the answer.

"It is whatever is in the path of a typhoon."

"Angel's father said we will get a direct hit," she continued.

"That is what I heard, too."

"Will our roof blow off, Daddy?"

"No, I don't think so. This is a well-built house. It's probably been through many typhoons."

That night, as Jenny fed Puppy her rice and sardines, she asked, "May Puppy sleep inside tonight? Please?" she begged.

"I think she'll be OK. She always finds a place to keep dry when it rains," her mom answered.

Very early the next morning, Jenny awoke to the sound of something slamming against the house. She saw her mom and dad hurrying past her bedroom door with towels and buckets.

"What is it?" Jenny cried, jumping out of bed and running after her parents. In the spare room in the back corner of the upstairs, water was running down the wall from under the closed windows, making a huge puddle on the floor.

"The typhoon is here," her mom answered.

"Banana plants grow up and put out one humongous bunch of bananas and after that they are cut down. New banana plants come up around older plants. How many kinds of bananas have you tasted? Here in the Philippines I have eaten six kinds and my dad says there are probably more than fifty different kinds."

—Jenny

TYPHOON

Jenny's mom was soaking up water from a windowsill. She squeezed out the towel into a bucket. Jenny's dad was doing the same thing. Even with the windows closed, the newly washed curtains were dripping wet. "I'll know next time not to wash curtains before a typhoon," Mom muttered. She left a folded towel on the sill and began mopping up water from the floor.

Jenny folded her arms around herself and shuddered. It was cold. The wind was howling. The house shook. A sudden loud crash against the wall made her jump. She looked at her dad.

"I think it's only rain being blown against the house by the strong wind," he said. Something slammed again. They heard a creaking sound.

"I don't like it," Jenny said. She was shaking all over.

"Go get dressed, Jenny," her mom said. "Then go in David's room and stay with him. I don't think the rain is coming in, yet, on that side of the house."

"I'll check the other windows," her father said, heading across the hall. "Just a minute, Davy, boy. Your sister will come and play with you. Don't climb out of your crib."

"Eat now," David said.

"Sorry, not yet. We're busy."

"Ta Tala make bweak'est?"

"She can't come today. It's raining too hard."

Jenny stopped in the hall. She noticed the painting they'd bought from the door-to-door salesman. It showed people working in rice fields outside a Filipino village. "Oh, Daddy," she wailed. "What will happen to the people living in houses made of mat walls and thatched roofs?"

"*Nipa* (*nee*-pah) huts? We can only pray for them, and for everyone," he added. "Go get dressed."

Jenny started to go into her room. Then remembered Puppy. Where was Puppy? Frantically she ran back into the hall. "Mom, Dad, Puppy is outside in the typhoon," she screamed.

"Puppy's OK," called her father. "I let her in. She beelined into that corner under the stairs. She's soaked, but I gave her the little rug Mom keeps in front of the sink."

"Get dressed now," Mom spoke up again. "You'll catch cold."

Knowing her puppy was safe, but feeling like almost nothing else was, Jenny pulled on whatever clothes her shaking hands grabbed. The wind was howling, and the slams against the side of the house were coming one after the other. Before she could remember what she was supposed to do next, her mother came into her room and set down a whimpering David.

"Take him downstairs, Jenny. The rain is starting to come under the window in his room now. Get out that box of Fruity-O's we bought in Manila to have for a special treat. You and Davy go ahead and eat them. Neither Dad nor I can stop mopping to cook breakfast.

Hearing a treat was coming, David went into the hall, turned around, and started backing carefully down the steps as he'd been taught to do.

Jenny hurried on ahead. A whining noise came from under the stairs, but Puppy would not come out when Jenny called her.

Because there were only three windows downstairs and they were all under overhangs, it was almost dark. Jenny flipped on the light switch. Nothing. *Oh, of course,* she thought. *Electricity would not be on in a typhoon.* She felt grown up for thinking of that. She also remembered to open and close the refrigerator door quickly when she took out the milk so food would stay cold as long as possible.

David climbed into his high chair, and Jenny fixed his cereal. It was almost like she was the mother. She wondered if Angel felt like this. She took care of her little brother most of the time. "What about Angel and her family?" Jenny asked out loud. David was stuffing his mouth with cereal he hadn't tasted in a long time. She continued, "Angel said their roof was leaking the last time it rained all those days. Her father was going to fix it as soon as he got the money." Jenny had not heard any pounding.

It was then that Jenny realized she was not hearing the wind's howling any more. She ran to one of the windows and cranked it open. It was barely raining. But where were the banana plants? For weeks Jenny had been watching their tops rise from behind the wall, as the plants grew taller. Each plant had put out one giant bunch of small green bananas that were slowly getting larger. Now she could not see one leaf above the wall.

"I think there's going to be lots of damage from this typhoon," her dad was saying as he and Mom walked down the stairs.

"Is it over?" Jenny asked.

"Just for a bit," replied her dad. "Pretty soon we'll be getting more of it. Did you know, Jenny, that typhoons look something like the picture in your science book of our Milky Way galaxy? The arms spin slowly around. Wind and rain come in waves as each arm moves by."

Jenny hadn't known that, but all she wanted was for the whole thing to pass them and be gone.

"I'll make coffee," Mom said, getting out her little aluminum pot. "I'm glad we have a couple of gas burners on our stove, and that our gas tank is full." She turned on the faucet to fill the coffee pot. "Oh no, no water!" she moaned.

"Everything's under control," Dad said, coming from the back room. "I made sure all our extra buckets were filled last night."

"Oh, thank you for remembering," Jenny's mother said. "Would you kids like a cup of hot chocolate?" For the hot chocolate, Mom got water from the filtered-water bucket. "You'd better keep this top bucket filled, Dear," Mom continued. "Because of the typhoon, I'd better use filtered water, even for cooking."

Jenny felt good. Her parents were both here, taking care of each other and her brother and her. She couldn't help thinking about Angel's family. Their mother was gone. Their roof leaked. They had only a tiny wood cook stove. Could *Nanay* find wood during a typhoon to make a fire?

Just as they finished their food and warm drinks, the typhoon hit again. The wind howled and the rain slammed against the front side of the house this time. Mom and Dad hurried upstairs.

ANGEL'S TREE

The next morning, sounds of pounding could be heard in several different directions. Rain continued off and on for days. Jenny thought she could not stand the musty smell of wet laundry one more minute. Even in her own bedroom, wet clothes on crisscrossed lines hung in her face wherever she turned. She felt cold. She wished they had a heater.

Even though people in town had started playing Christmas music and putting up decorations before All Saints' Day, Jenny's mother said they couldn't get theirs out until after Thanksgiving. Filipinos didn't celebrate American Thanksgiving, but missionaries had had sort of a Thanksgiving meal together. It had not seemed like Thanksgiving to Jenny. It wasn't fall. There was no turkey. No cranberry sauce. But, all the food was American—chicken and gravy, stuffing, mashed potatoes, and pies—not exactly apple or pumpkin—but sort of like them. Then the typhoon came.

Now, finally, the sun was shining. *Ka* Tala had come back to work right after the typhoon, but not *Ate*, because she had to take late afternoon classes. Jenny hadn't seen any of Angel's family since the typhoon, but today she was too excited to think about them. Mom said they could get out their Christmas decorations.

"Where are they, Mom? May I get them out?"

"They're right there on the table," Mom answered.

Jenny stared at the small box. "That's all?" She didn't believe it. Back home they'd had many boxes of decorations. It took almost all day to put them around the house.

"I know it's not very much," Mom said with a big sigh. "But have you forgotten how hard it was to fit our things into the packing boxes when we got ready to come last summer?"

"But…" Jenny's lip quivered, and tears began rolling down her cheeks. It was just so, so sad. Nothing was the same. Not even decorating for Christmas was any fun!

"We'd planned," Mom continued, "for all of us to go to Manila for a weekend. We were going to stay at the mission home and go Christmas shopping together in the malls. But because of the typhoon and all, the busses and stores are just too crowded for us all to go now."

"I really don't like typhoons," Jenny said, more tears coming. "Everything stops."

"Actually, I'm planning to go to Manila on Saturday, Jenny."

"You're going without Daddy?" Jenny couldn't believe it. Her mom had not gone anywhere alone since they'd come.

"Two other ladies from the language school and I want to go Christmas shopping."

"Oh good," Jenny said, relieved.

"But," Mom continued, "we can buy only what we can carry home on very crowded busses, Jenny."

All the same, feeling better, Jenny took the few familiar decorations out of the box. It was nice to see the centerpiece they always used on their dining room table, and she enjoyed carefully unwrapping each of the special ornaments they'd collected. "You just have to buy a tree, Mom," Jenny said.

"I really don't think I can, Jenny. I hear they are expensive, and I can't imagine how I could carry one in the small Manila taxis, then all the way home on the bus. It's very hard even to get a ride at this time of year."

Disappointed and discouraged, Jenny went up to her room. The sun was beginning to make her feel hot and sweaty again. She opened her window. Looking out, she saw Angel with a towel over her head, pretending to chase her little brother. *Totoy* was running and screaming. Except for the little airplane *Totoy* was given when his mom left, Jenny had never seen either one of them playing with a real toy.

Just then, Angel pulled the towel off her head and looked up at Jenny. She smiled and waved and motioned for her to come over. Jenny's mom was staying home from school this morning to get caught up, now that the sun was out. Jenny ran down the stairs. "Mom, Angel is asking me over. May I go?"

"I don't know if her mother would want you over there, now that she's away."

"Oh, I know it's OK," Jenny answered quickly. "She likes me."

"And how do you know that?" Mom asked, her eyebrows rising.

"That day I went on the *jeepney* to Manila, Angel's mother said she liked me being Angel's friend. She said I looked like an American high schooler who was kind to her a long time ago."

"You did say once that Angel's mother worked for missionaries in Manila, didn't you, Jenny?" Mom asked.

"Yes, at a missionary kids' school, when *Ate* was a baby."

Mom looked thoughtful. "Let's see," she said, looking up at the ceiling, "that would have been about fifteen years ago. I wonder… What did this kind girl you look like do for Angel's mother?"

"She helped her with her work so she could stay home longer on the weekend with her children. Mom! You told me once you did that for someone, remember? Was that girl you?"

"My goodness!" Mom exclaimed.

"May I go now? I have to tell Angel."

"OK, Jenny. Be back by noon."

Familiar Christmas songs were coming from a stereo just inside the open door of Angel's house. Across from the doorway, Jenny saw a small bush propped up on a low table. Red paper bows and bits of colored tinsel decorated the drooping branches.

"Do you like our Christmas tree?" Angel asked, smiling.

Jenny looked at the bush. She could not think of what to say.

Angel went on, "*Ate* get before typhoon coming to our place. We know it not last up to Christmas, but we like now still." Angel's eyes were bright with excitement, and *Totoy* danced around the room.

Finally, Jenny spoke. "We have a few decorations. And my mother is going to Manila on Saturday to do her Christmas shopping." Even while she was saying the words, Jenny wondered what Angel would think. Her family probably didn't have money for Christmas shopping.

"*Inay* send money, but *Tiyo* Romy say he need. I think next time money come, maybe we able to keep. *Tatay* say, when money come, he fix our roof. When typhoon come, it very hard for us." The corners of Angel's mouth turned way down. *Totoy* stopped dancing and looked up at Jenny with the same sad expression on his little face.

Jenny looked around the room, wondering what to say. She remembered the book she'd given to Angel. "Did you like the book I gave you?"

"Yes, I like so much. I read four times."

"Are you going to school now, Angel?"

"I will attend again next summer already."

"But I thought you were going back soon," Jenny said, surprised.

"*Ate* not able support my need. She say it take all her money buying our food."

Disappointed, Jenny asked, "What about your father? Doesn't he buy your food?"

"Yes. He buy. And sometime, *Kuya*. And sometime, *Nanay*. Everybody help."

The talk about food seemed to remind *Totoy* about eating. He began fussing and begging. Angel went into the room with the dirt floor but came right back out and said, "Go find *Nanay, Totoy*. She at her store." *Totoy* ran out the front door.

Jenny had run out of things to say. She had lots of questions but was afraid she'd already asked too many. She really liked Angel and didn't want to embarrass her. But now that *Totoy* was gone, Angel did not seem to know what to do.

"Would you like to come over to my house?" Jenny asked.

Angel's face brightened. "I tell *Nanay*. It not be hard for her. After *Totoy* eat, he sleep. Come." She grabbed Jenny's hand and pulled her out the door and toward *Nanay's* sari-sari store near the street.

Jenny wasn't sure what her mother was going to say about inviting Angel without asking first, but when they got back to her house, her mom was busy upstairs. Jenny got out cookies and drinks; then after their *merienda*, they went up to Jenny's room. Like last time, Jenny liked watching Angel play. Everything was new to her. Angel stayed for lunch and for most of the afternoon. When she was leaving, she spoke to Jenny's mom, "I go now, Ma'am. I love your place. So much pretty thing for Christmas."

Coming inside after seeing Angel out the gate, Jenny remembered she'd been so shocked by Angel's tree she'd forgotten all about telling her their mothers knew each other long ago. "So much pretty thing?" Jenny repeated Angel's words as she stared at the few ornaments on the table. "Mom."

"Yes, Dear."

"Angel has something she calls a Christmas tree. But it's only a dead bush with paper bows on it."

"Oh? They certainly don't seem to have much. The way Angel ate at lunch, I wondered if she hadn't eaten breakfast."

"I don't think she had, Mom. When *Totoy* wanted a snack, Angel couldn't find anything to give him. And she's not going to school either."

"But I thought Ana told her she'd buy what she needed."

"She couldn't. Angel said they needed all the money for food," Jenny explained. "May we help them, Mom?"

"We can't help everybody, Jenny. Hundreds of families here have the same needs."

"But we could help one of the families, Mom, couldn't we?"

THE IDEA

It was almost dark, and Jenny's mom wasn't back from Manila. Dad had walked to the corner several times, hoping to see a *trike* coming. "I'd like to go into town and wait at the bus stop," he'd said to no one in particular a half hour ago, "but I can't leave the kids here alone. No telling we'd even find each other anyway." Dad went outside and stood by the gate, looking up the dark street. Jenny and David joined him in the warm December evening.

"What are we going to do?" Jenny asked, feeling her dad's helplessness.

Dad sighed loudly. "I wish Jo Jo were around," he answered. "I'd send him in there to the bus stop; so when Mom gets off the bus, she could get a ride home with someone she knows."

"Do you know Angel's father, Daddy?" Jenny asked.

"Your mom and I have ridden to the language school a few times in Jo Jo's *trike*."

Jenny remembered the day before the typhoon when she and *Ka* Tala were stuck at the open market. All the *trikes* were busy, and they'd not known how they'd ever get a ride home. How thankful they'd been when Angel's father stopped to pick them up in his *trike*! *Yes, it would be great if Angel's father came by right now.*

Suddenly, the lights went out all over the neighborhood. Jenny's dad gave another big sigh. "That's all Mom needs," he said. "It's impossible to tell where to ask the bus to stop if there are no lights in town. She could end up getting off in the wrong place and not knowing where she is."

"Let's pray, Daddy." Jenny said.

"Pay," echoed Davy, reaching up his arms to his dad.

Dad bent down and picked up Davy, then started to pray. It was very dark. Jenny looked up at the sky. When the electricity was off, the stars were easy to see. She saw the Big Dipper and the Southern Cross. Going outside to look at the night sky was a fun thing their family had done together when the electricity went off in the evening.

Jenny was certain her mother was having trouble. She didn't know what kind, but she knew her dad was really worried. She told God she didn't care about Christmas anymore, only that her mother would come home safely. Jenny knew it was because of her that her mom had dared to go to Manila without her dad. Her mom was trying to make a nice Christmas for her. She wished she hadn't been so selfish. Maybe now her mother would never come home.

But what is that? wondered Jenny.

They all heard the faraway sound of a *trike*. It came closer, turned at the corner, and stopped in front of their house. Jenny followed her dad out the gate. Her mom was inside the *trike*. "Mom!" Jenny yelled, not meaning to. One of the missionary men from the language school was sitting on the back of the driver's seat behind the driver. Setting Davy down and handing his flashlight to Jenny, Dad picked up the plastic bags from the floor around Mom's feet. Mom collected the ones on the seat beside her and climbed out. The missionary took a big box off the back and set it on the patio inside the open gate.

"Thanks a lot, Jim," Dad said, shaking the missionary's hand. Jim got inside the *trike*, the driver turned it around, and they started back toward town.

"All three of us ladies took a *trike* together from the bus stop to Ann Brown's house, because it was the closest," Mom said.

"That must have been some loaded *trike*," exclaimed Dad, walking across the patio toward the house. "Open the door for me, Jenny."

"Then," Mom continued explaining, "Ann's husband, Jim, brought me home, and now he's going back to his house to ride home with Sue. It's all worked out OK."

"I'm sure thankful you didn't have to travel alone after dark," Dad said. Jenny heard bumps and rattles, as her dad set the bags down on the hard floor inside the dark house. "Jenny, give me the flashlight, please," he said. "Everybody wait out there 'till I get a candle lit. How did you ladies know where to get off the bus in the dark?" Dad called out to Mom.

"That was a worry," Mom answered. "We prayed. What else could we do? So many people were standing in the aisle, we couldn't go up front to ask the driver where we were, especially trying to hang on to all our stuff. Then a man near us heard us talking and told us when it was our stop. How he could see, I'm sure I don't know! We had to trust that he was right."

"We prayed, and after that we heard the *trike* coming," Jenny said.

"I knew you would be praying," Mom said, "and it was a big help to me." She set her bags down by the door and went back to pick up the box and close and lock the gate.

Dad had just lit the candle when the lights came back on. While he and Mom were trying to hug each other with David clinging between them, Jenny looked at the heap of bulging plastic bags and at a picture of a Christmas tree on the big box. When she finally had a turn for a hug, Jenny said, "I told God all I wanted was for you to come home safely, Mom."

David spied something interesting in one of the bags. "No, no, no," Dad said, scooping him up. "It's time you got ready for bed, little man. You, too, Jenny," he added. "Let's go upstairs."

Jenny knew her parents didn't want her to look in any of the bags, and that was OK. Everything was OK, except... Now that Mom was safely home, what about the problem of Angel's Christmas?

After church the next day, while she was changing into play clothes, Jenny looked around her room wondering what she could give to Angel. Not Charlotte. Not her little music box. Maybe another book, maybe a craft kit, maybe something to wear, maybe...

"Jenny," her father called from the bottom of the stairs, "hurry up, Mom has lunch ready."

As Jenny pulled out a chair to join her family, already seated at the table, her mom was talking. "...and it was so hot in Manila. Christmas music and decorations just didn't feel right." After Jenny's dad said the blessing, Mom continued, "I can't get into Christmas at all. I don't—"

"May we set up the tree after lunch, Mom?" Jenny cut in.

"Don't interrupt, Jenny." Mom said abruptly. "You've been taught better than that."

"Sorry, Mom," Jenny apologized.

"Anyway, you won't be very happy with the tree," Mom went on. "It's a lot smaller than the nice one we had back home." Mom rested her head in her hands.

Dad looked at Mom. "Jenny and I will clean up lunch and set up the tree, Dear. Why don't you go ahead and take a nap today with Davy?"

"I guess I'll do that," she answered. "Thanks."

After Mom and Davy had gone upstairs, Dad put water on the stove to heat for washing dishes. As Jenny cleared the table, she asked, "What's wrong with Mom, Daddy?"

"She's tired from her trip yesterday. And she misses her family and friends, and the winter weather. She thinks about the things we were able to do back home at Christmas time. And language study is not the easiest thing in the world, or trying to live with so many inconveniences and changes. Actually, I feel the same way," Dad ended. It was almost like her dad had forgotten he'd been talking to her.

The lid on the water kettle began to rattle. Jenny's dad turned off the gas and dumped the boiling water into the dishpans in the sink. He added soap to one pan, dropped in the silverware then added a little cold water. They worked in silence except for the sound of the dishes scraping against the metal washbasins.

"Do you feel like setting up the Christmas tree, Daddy?" Jenny asked as they finished.

"Sure, I'll do it. I don't know what your mother bought. Let's go look."

Jenny dug into one of the plastic bags her mom had left on the couch. "Oh good, Mom bought lights," she exclaimed. "Daddy, if you'll put the tree together and string the lights on it, I'll finish," Jenny said.

"Fine," Dad agreed. "That will give me a little time for a nap myself."

Dad laid the parts of the tree on the floor and started putting the branches into the holes in the trunk. "You probably don't realize, Jenny, how hard it must have been for Mom to carry all this stuff home on the crowded busses. I really don't know how she did it. Be sure to tell her how much you appreciate it."

"I will, Daddy. I do appreciate it a whole bunch, and most of all I'm so glad she got home safely, aren't you?"

"I sure am," Dad replied as he headed up the stairs.

The tree was small, but Jenny liked it. What if all they had was an old bush like Angel's family? What if they were Angel's family?

That gave Jenny an idea. Even though their Christmas wasn't going to be anything like usual, it would be so much more than Angel's! What if they pretended Angel's family was part of their family? What if they gave her family the same kind of Christmas they were going to have?

Jenny worked hard, trimming the tree with the ornaments they'd brought from home and the few new things from Manila. Mom had bought a set of really cute little painted snowmen to hang on the tree. Jenny was surprised that Filipinos had snowmen decorations. Just like she'd been surprised to hear "Frosty the Snowman" and "White Christmas" played over the radio. She wondered how snow could be connected to a hot Philippine Christmas.

Jenny hurried. She wanted the tree to be all ready when her family came downstairs. She hoped they would think it was pretty. And she couldn't wait to tell them about her idea for Angel's family.

JENNY'S TREE

"Oh, how nice," Jenny's mom exclaimed as she came slowly down the stairs with David. Because it was getting dark and Jenny had not turned on other lights, the tree lights made the ornaments and tinsel sparkle. "It is a pretty little tree," Mom added.

David, who didn't remember other Christmases, was totally awed. He pointed and couldn't say anything that made sense.

Then Dad came down. "Very nice, Jenny," he said, giving her a big hug.

Jenny was happy and satisfied with the effect of her efforts. Was this a good time to tell everyone her idea? No, she decided. She would wait until after supper when they'd probably sit down together to enjoy the new Christmas tree. She hoped the electricity would not go off.

"You know what?" Mom called from the kitchen, where she'd turned on a light to start supper. "I bought something else to go with the tree. It must be in one of the other bags. If you'll get stuff out for sandwiches," she said to Jenny's dad, "I'll go upstairs and find it."

In a minute, she was back with a flat box. She handed it to Jenny.

Jenny looked at the picture on the box. "It's a manger scene just like we had back home!" she exclaimed.

"It is exactly like it, except smaller," Mom said. "Ours at home was so old. I didn't know they still sold them."

"Well, look at that," Dad said, coming back from the kitchen and taking one end of the box in his hand to look at the picture. "I'm so glad Mom found this. Here, Jenny," he said, taking out his pocketknife and slitting the tape holding the box shut. "I'll put the walls and roof together and attach the star, and you put the figures in those little lift-up things on the bottom."

After the manger scene was together and sitting on the floor under the tree, Jenny's dad found a bulb toward the bottom of the string of Christmas lights and placed it into a hole behind the star. Its light shown down on Baby Jesus and his mother, just the way it had on the manger scene they'd left packed away back home.

"Now that is really nice," Mom said, setting a plate of sandwiches on the coffee table.

"Let's sing 'Away in a Manger' before I thank Jesus for our food," Dad suggested. Even Davy sang—a few words behind the others. He'd been listening to Jenny sing along with her Christmas tapes and was learning some of the words.

Right after Mom brought in the cookies, Jenny said, "Mommy and Daddy, I have an idea I hope you will like."

"What is your idea, Pun'kin?" Dad asked.

"Well, Angel's mother is gone, you know. She sent money once, but Angel's uncle took it. Their roof leaked terribly in the typhoon, and Angel said they hardly have any money to buy food. They have a bush for a

Christmas tree, but it won't even last up to Christmas." Jenny paused and took a deep breath. "Could we pretend they are part of our family for Christmas? Could we give them the same things we will have? I know ours will be small this year, but I don't think they will have any Christmas at all." Jenny came to the end of everything she had thought out. With a little smile on her lips, she turned pleading eyes toward her mom and dad.

"Well," her dad began slowly, "I'm not sure what they would like."

"Sometimes different people need different things than other people," Mom added. "We've been given a few ideas about gifts at the language school. And, there's *Ka* Tala, too, you know. Our house girl guidelines suggest a certain amount of money to spend on a Christmas gift for her."

"Then we will give to *Ate*, too. She used to work for us," Jenny spoke up.

Jenny's dad put his hand up and rubbed his chin. He turned to her mom. "Do you think you could find out from Tala what would be the right thing to do for Angel's family?"

"I can ask," Mom answered then looked at Jenny. "We don't have a lot of money, you know, but we'll try to find out what we can do."

Jenny jumped up and hugged her parents. "Thank you so much, Mom, for all the things you bought and carried home on the bus," she said, giving her mom an extra-long hug. David, seeing her excitement, jumped up and hugged everybody. Mom and Dad seemed happy now, too. It would be a good Christmas.

When *Ka* Tala arrived the next morning, Jenny ached to ask her about Christmas, but Mom and Dad said they'd find out. Jenny tried her hardest to control herself.

"What you excited about?" *Ka* Tala asked as soon as she saw her. Then she spotted the Christmas tree. "Oh, you getting ready for Christmas now!" she exclaimed.

"Yes," Jenny answered, smiling. Thinking of a question she hoped would be OK, she asked, "*Ka* Tala, what is your favorite thing for Christmas?"

"For us," began *Ka* Tala, "when Christmas coming, everyone forgive each other. The ones who fighting try to get along—for sake of Christ Child. When we sitting to our meal together on *Noche Buena*—midnight Christmas Eve—the whole family, we are peaceful. For me, it the best thing."

Ka Tala's answer was not what Jenny could have guessed. She thought about it as she went upstairs to make her bed. She looked out her window to see if Angel was outside. She was. Like almost every morning, she was laying wet clothes on the bushes. *Ate* Ana, dressed in her school uniform, was just climbing into a *trike*. Jenny didn't see *Totoy*.

Jenny called from her window, "Hi, Angel."

"*Hoy*, Jenny," Angel responded, looking up and waving.

"Would you like to come over?" Jenny called. "I want to show you something."

"OK, I come," Angel answered, disappearing around the corner.

Jenny knew she was going to their *sari-sari* store to tell her grandmother. She hurried downstairs and out to the front gate to meet her.

"Wait right here just a minute," she told Angel after letting her in and relocking the gate. Jenny ran inside and plugged in the tree lights. Even during the day, they looked pretty.

"Come on in now," Jenny said, holding open the screen door for Angel. She pulled her around the corner into their *sala*.

"Oh," Angel whispered, rounding her mouth and laying her hands on her cheeks. She walked slowly toward the tree and knelt down close to the manger scene. "Holy Mother and the Christ Child," she said reverently. Jenny was surprised to see her kiss her fingers and rest them gently on the figures. After a minute Angel stood up and looked at the tree. Jenny watched to see what she would think. "You have many cute Frosty," she said, gently touching each one.

"I don't think Mom would mind if I gave you one of them," Jenny said hesitantly, looking at *Ka* Tala who was dusting the *sala* chairs. *Ka* Tala said nothing. "Which one would you like?" Jenny asked Angel.

"I not want," Angel answered, as she touched the other ornaments.

Jenny's mother had said the snowmen weren't really expensive. "It's OK, Angel. I want you to have one," she said again.

"I not take," Angel said.

Jenny was puzzled and hurt. The sadness she felt because Angel wouldn't accept a gift she truly wanted to give her showed on her face.

Ka Tala stood up and came near. "You choose, Jenny," she said.

"She doesn't want one, *Ka* Tala."

"I think this good," *Ka* Tala said, removing one from the tree and putting it in Jenny's hand.

Confused, Jenny held it out to Angel. Angel smiled and took the little snowman. Quickly running a finger over the tiny broom he carried, she slipped the ornament into her pocket. She said nothing.

"Come, Jenny, we make *merienda* for your friend." *Ka* Tala took Jenny's hand and headed to the kitchen. "Sit there, Angel," she said, pointing with her lip to a chair at the table.

As they were eating cookies, they heard David calling from his room upstairs. He'd been fussy, so Jenny's mom had asked *Ka* Tala to give him a morning nap. She went up to get him.

"Where is *Totoy* today, Angel?" Jenny asked.

"He stay to house of *Tiya* Nene."

Angel had told Jenny before that her mother's sister Nene didn't get along with their family. She remembered the time she'd heard yelling across the street. When she'd looked out her window, she'd seen Angel's mother and another woman slapping each other with their *chinelas*—their flip-flops. The woman was *Tiya* Nene, because Jenny had met her the day they took Angel's mother to Manila.

"How come *Totoy* is with her?" Jenny asked, surprised.

"It like I tell you, Jenny, "*Ka* Tala answered for Angel as she came down the stairs with David. "When Christmas coming, family try to get along. It big help to *Nanay*."

"Oh," Jenny said, remembering.

After *merienda*, Angel said her grandmother needed her, and she left. Usually she stayed longer. Jenny wondered what was wrong. "*Ka* Tala, I don't know... I thought..." She tried to think how to express her confusion. "I thought Angel would like to have a snowman, but I guess she didn't really care."

"Oh, she want, Jenny," *Ka* Tala answered quickly.

"She said she didn't."

"But you say only two time."

"What?" Jenny asked, even more confused.

"Filipinos want to know you really serious. They never take when only mention two time."

"And..." Jenny hesitated, hoping it was OK to say it, "Angel didn't say 'thank you' when I gave it to her."

"She not say 'thank you' to friend, maybe."

"Why?" Jenny asked. "It's not polite not to say 'thank you.'"

"Most probably Angel forget only. She thinking you always nice, Jenny. Sometime Angel give you little gift. It showing she like."

"I know Angel doesn't have money."

"If Filipino not have money, they borrow for important thing."

Ka Tala turned and went to the kitchen to fix *merienda* for David. She seemed to be through talking. Jenny had one more question, but she would have to wait to find out why Angel put a kiss on their manger scene figure of Mary and Baby Jesus. And again she'd forgotten to tell Angel about their mothers' knowing each other a long time ago. Hearing about that would make Angel happy, she was sure.

At noon, when Jenny's mom and dad came home from language school, they brought two big boxes that had arrived in the mail that morning.

PACKAGES FROM BACK HOME

———— ❧ ————

"What is it?" Jenny asked excitedly.

"We don't know," Dad answered, "but one is from Grandma, and the other is from the church."

"They must be for Christmas," Mom said.

Jenny took a closer look at the packages. Yes, there was her grandmother's return address on one and the pastor's on the other. "May we open them now?" she asked.

"We have a big test tomorrow," her dad said, "so if you kids are quiet, and we get our studying done this afternoon, we can open them after supper."

"Goodie," Jenny said, jumping up and down and clapping her hands.

"Goodie," copied David, trying to jump up and down, but only lifting up one foot at a time. They all laughed.

"You're silly, Davy," Jenny said, giving him a hug.

"Dad and I will have to check the boxes first, though," Mom added, "in case something isn't wrapped."

"Will we have homeschool?" Jenny asked.

"I think not," Mom answered. "We're ahead, and I'd better not take the time this afternoon. Why don't you work on another craft kit? You still have a couple left, haven't you?"

Glad not to have school and excited about the packages, Jenny happily went to her room after lunch. But in a few minutes, just when she'd decided which kit to open, her mom called, "Jenny, you'll have to play with David for me. After taking that long nap this morning, he's not going to sleep and I need *Ka* Tala to keep working on the cleaning."

Jenny put the kit back on the shelf and went into her brother's room. "What do you want to do, Davy?" she asked.

"Pay," he answered, going toward his toy box. Then a book lying on top caught his eye. "Weed to me?" he asked, holding out the board book and looking hopeful.

Staying with her little brother all afternoon wasn't exactly fun, but David had lots of things to play with. Sometimes he even played by himself. When he was occupied, Jenny could at least read, as long as she stayed in the room with him. Finally, Mom said they could come downstairs.

After supper, Jenny's dad set the two packages on the dining room table. He took out his pocketknife and slit the tape along the top edges of the boxes. "They arrived in pretty good shape for all the way they've come," he commented. "Now, you kids go into the *sala* and sit on the couch while Mom and I have a quick look first."

Jenny took David's hand, and they went together to wait on the couch. Jenny looked at their little tree and at the manger scene. "Dad," she called, remembering the strange thing Angel had done with it.

"Wait a minute," Dad answered. "Your mom has to take a few things upstairs first."

"But I need to ask you something," Jenny continued.

"Just a minute," he called back.

They saw their mother carry a bag of things up the stairs.

"Now you may come," their dad said.

In a second they'd scooted off the couch. Both were running across the slippery, waxed marble floor toward the table when Jenny heard a crash. Looking back, she saw David on the floor. His face looked like he was crying, but he wasn't making a sound. Jenny felt terrified.

"I got him," Dad called out to Mom who was hurrying down the stairs. Dad scooped up David and bounced him against his shoulder. "It's OK, Buddy," he said, patting his back. Finally, Davy gasped and began crying loudly.

"Did he hit his head hard?" Mom asked, rubbing the back of David's head, trying to comfort him. "Oh, it's his lip," she said suddenly. "He has blood all over his chin and on your shirt. Check his mouth," she said to Jenny's dad, as she went toward the kitchen sink and started running cold water on a clean rag.

"Everything looks OK inside," Dad said, handing a sobbing David to Mom, who sat down and started gently wiping away the blood. Dad took off his shirt and rinsed the bloody place out under the faucet, then headed up the stairs. "Do you want me to bring down Davy's sleepers?" he called.

"Yes. He's really tired. He didn't take a nap this afternoon."

"Mom," Jenny started. No one had said anything to her the whole time. She was afraid she'd caused her brother to fall. She was also remembering when *Totoy* had wiped out on the waxed cement floors in his house. His mother had been there that time, but now… "Mom, I…"

"It's OK, Jenny," Mom said, seeing Jenny's worried face. "Davy will be OK. She put an arm around her and gave her a gentle hug.

"Mom, what if *Totoy* got hurt like Davy?" Jenny wondered out loud. "Did you know he's staying with Angel's aunt? And she doesn't like their mother. I saw them hitting each other once."

"You did?" Jenny's mom seemed surprised. "Why is *Totoy* not staying at home?"

"I don't know, except *Ka* Tala said at Christmas time all the family tries to be nice to each other. She said, '…because of the Christ Child.' What does that mean, Mom?"

"I'm not sure."

"And, do you know what Angel did to our manger scene?" Jenny finally had a chance to ask. "She kissed her fingers and touched Mary and Baby Jesus. She called Mary 'Holy Mother.'"

"We'll talk about that sometime, Jenny. Remind me, OK? By the way, I asked about things we could do for their family for Christmas, and I have some ideas."

"What are we going to give them?" Jenny asked excitedly.

"After tomorrow's language test, we can plan it out," Mom answered. "Then on Saturday, if Dad can watch David for a while, you and I will go to the open market and do some shopping, OK?"

"Yes. That will be so fun, Mom." Jenny couldn't wait. "I hope we can give them the same nice Christmas we're going to have—just like they were part of our own family."

In a minute her dad was back, wearing a clean shirt and carrying David's PJ's. "I'll dress Davy," he said, picking him up off Mom's lap where he'd almost fallen asleep. "You two go ahead and take the things out of those boxes."

As Jenny and her mom lifted out beautifully wrapped packages and laid them carefully on the table, Jenny began to notice something. Each package with the name of someone in her family on it had a matching package with no name on it. "Who are these for?" Jenny asked.

"Which ones, Dear?"

Her mom must not have seen what Jenny had noticed. "Mom, look." Jenny started arranging the packages in sets. "One package in each set has a blank name tag."

"Well, I don't know," her mom responded, looking more closely at the gift tags. "I wish Pastor's wife had enclosed a note. You didn't see one, did you, Jenny?" They began stirring around the newspaper packing. Then they took it all out of the box, flattening each piece. "It's a mystery, isn't it?" Mom said. "Maybe they'll send us a letter. There're still a few more days 'till Christmas."

"The packages from Grandma only came in ones," commented Jenny. "May I put them under our tree?"

"Actually, it's a pretty small area, don't you think?" Mom said, smiling. Jenny had to admit that was true. "Anyway," Mom concluded, "it would be best to wait until Christmas Eve."

"But just a few? One for each of us?" Jenny tried again.

"No," Mom stated, standing up and starting to put the packages back into the boxes. "You need to get ready for bed now, Jenny."

"That's right," Jenny's dad said, coming downstairs from tucking David in. "Your mom and I still have a little more studying to do. Can you put yourself to bed tonight, Pun'kin?" he asked Jenny.

"OK, Daddy." Jenny hugged and kissed both her parents and went upstairs. Why would the church have sent doubles of all their presents, she wondered? Jenny fell asleep thinking about the plans they would make tomorrow and the shopping trip with her mom on Saturday. She had never been to the market with her mom, only with *Ka* Tala. Did her mom know how to shop in the open market?

"I ride in *tricycles* when we go to the market, to church or to other places in town. Do you think you would like to ride in one? There are many *trikes*, but when a typhoon is coming or it's starting to get dark, everybody wants to get home and it's hard to find an empty one."

—Jenny

SHOPPING WITH MOM

"Now," Jenny's mom began when they'd finally finished their homeschool lessons for the day, "here's a list of things they said Filipinos like for Christmas."

Jenny looked at the list her mom laid on the table. "Spaghetti?" she asked.

"It's one of their favorites. And they use hot dogs and catsup in it."

"Angel likes banana catsup," Jenny added.

"Oh, that's right. Help me remember to buy that kind." Mom picked up the list and looked down through it. "They like fruit cocktail for their *buko*—young coconut—salad and sweetened condensed milk and evaporated milk and mayonnaise—"

"Angel said once her father bought her an apple for Christmas," Jenny interrupted.

"Yes, apples—don't interrupt, Jenny—and grapes, too, are a special treat, as they are for us here in the Philippines. But I don't know if we can find any in our market. In Manila I bought a couple cheese balls. We can decide whether to give them or keep them. And Filipinos also like canned hams and imported Hershey's Kisses. I don't know if we can find them here, either, and if we can, they may be too expensive."

"I saw Hershey bars in Cely's Pharmacy," Jenny said. "Is food what we are going to give Angel's family?"

"Mostly. We can give the food to Ana. That way they will think we are giving because she used to work for us, and they won't be embarrassed to take it. Ana will share with her whole family. Also, we'll make a basket of food for *Ka* Tala."

"May we buy toys for her children?" Jenny asked.

"I plan to give her money along with the food. She can use it any way she wants."

"Will we give money to Angel's family, too?"

"No. But your dad had an idea. I guess it's OK to tell you, but in no way can you ever tell Angel or anyone in her family. Promise?" Mom asked.

"I promise. But why?"

"First, I'll tell you what's going to happen. The pastor of the church we attend in town will use money we gave him to have Angel's family's roof fixed. He will not tell anyone where the money came from."

"Oh, Mom, I'm so glad," Jenny said, hugging her mom. "But why can't they know it's from us?" she asked, not understanding.

"Filipinos cannot accept help without giving something back. If they were not able to do something for us, they would feel so embarrassed they could never be friendly toward us again. This way Angel's family won't know who helped, so they can't feel they owe us. It's really important for you not to give any hint."

"Does *Ka* Tala know?"

"No. And you can't tell her, either. I hope I've not made a mistake by telling you."

"I promise I won't tell, Mom. I wouldn't like it at all if Angel and *Ate* Ana could not be my friends. When will their roof get fixed?"

"I don't know. Soon, we hope."

Just then a round of explosions interrupted their conversation. They both jumped and covered their ears. David started crying and calling from upstairs. "I will never get used to those firecrackers! They could give you a heart attack!" Mom exclaimed, getting up from the table and running up the stairs.

Jenny thought she was getting used to them, but they always ended up making her jump. She was beginning to dread them. They had started hearing small ones around All Saints' Day, and ever since, they'd become louder and louder. Sometimes they woke her from a sound sleep late at night. Angel had said that when New Year's Eve came, everyone in the Philippines would be setting off firecrackers. Jenny could not imagine what that would be like.

"There go some more," her mom said as she carried David downstairs. "Once they start, everybody has to add to it, it seems." Firecrackers could be heard close by, then farther and farther away.

Soon after eight o'clock the next day, Jenny and her mom climbed into a *trike*. Jenny hadn't ridden in one very much, but her mom and dad rode *trikes* to school and back every weekday. Loud music, mostly beating drums and noise, was coming from a speaker. She felt like covering her ears, but she didn't. Her mom took a cloth handkerchief from her pocket and held it over her mouth and nose like *Ka* Tala did sometimes.

Jenny didn't like the exhaust smells either. She wished the driver would not stay so close to the back of other *trikes*. She was glad when they reached the market.

After paying the driver, they went just inside the near corner of the market and bought two big baskets. "We'll use these to carry what we buy, and later we'll pack the Christmas gifts in them," Mom explained to Jenny. Then they started walking down the stall-lined street outside the enclosed market area. Mom held tightly onto Jenny's hand like *Ka* Tala did.

Jenny soon had some surprises. Sellers called out to her mother like they knew her. She stopped and talked with one lady and bought bananas from her. Then they ducked under several low hanging signs and walked along one of the dirt paths between stalls inside the market. Jenny had to keep an eye on the path to avoid holes and garbage, and to stay on the occasional little board-bridges. Once when she was with *Ka* Tala, she'd slipped on a muddy place and fallen into a ditch of *who knows what*—at least that's what Mom had called it when she got home. She hoped her mom wasn't headed to the meat section, because the mud there was the worst, and the smells made her feel sick.

"Oh, I see grapes and apples!" Jenny heard her mom exclaim quietly. Jenny looked up. Her mom continued, "They are expensive, I'm sure. I'll get just a few."

Jenny watched her mom arguing over the price in *Tagalog* just like *Ka* Tala. "I didn't know you knew how to do this," Jenny said to her as they left the vendor's table.

"Sometimes we come to the market during class to buy things and practice our *Tagalog*," her mom explained. "Now, the rest of what we want we'll find in the mini marts. Let's go over to this one first," she said, guiding Jenny away from the stalls, to the other side of the crowded street, and up the steps into the crowded store.

They checked their fresh things in at the counter just inside the entrance and picked up a store basket. Into the basket went two or more of each of the things on their list. "If there's something you want for us, I'll ask *Ka* Tala to pick it up on Monday," her mother said. "Can you think of anything else we should look for now?" Jenny almost did not hear her mother's question because of the loud noise made by so many people talking.

"Do you think we could buy a ham?" Jenny spoke up. She felt so grown up, shopping like this with her mother. "And what about candy?" she added.

"I'll ask when we get to the cash register."

Jenny was surprised again when she saw how her mother worked her way up to the checkout counter. The first time Jenny had gone to the store with *Ka* Tala, she'd been so embarrassed when *Ka* Tala pushed through the group to the counter. "If you stand in line everyone will go ahead of you," *Ka* Tala had explained. Like *Ka* Tala and the others, Jenny's mother did not wait very long in line.

"Are there canned hams?" her mother asked the lady at the checkout counter.

"Out of stock, Ma'am," the lady answered, turning the corners of her mouth way down.

"And are there Hershey's Kisses?" her mom asked, looking around, as if trying to see some.

"I will get." The lady called a girl standing nearby and spoke to her in fast *Tagalog*. "Only few minute, Ma'am. We get for you."

"Thank you," Jenny's mom said, "maybe another day." She paid for the groceries. Jenny knew there was no bargaining in the mini marts, but she was confused. Did her mom want to buy the candy or not? After they picked up their fresh things from the man near the door, she asked her.

"I didn't want to wait a long time then find out it's 'out of stock,' too," her mom explained. "Or have them going to another store to get some for me."

"Do you think she knew where to get some?" Jenny asked.

"She may have, but anyway, I'd like to know the price first. Which pharmacy was it where you saw the Hershey bars?"

"Cely's, the one way over by the building where the language school is."

"Oh, do you think we can make it? This stuff is getting awfully heavy," Mom said. Each of them was now carrying things in both hands. "If you'd rather not, we can skip it."

Mom was speaking to her like a grown-up, Jenny thought. "I want to try," she answered. But she really wasn't sure she could carry her things that far.

"Give me that heavy one," her mom said, pointing with her lower lip toward the plastic bags in Jenny's right hand. Mom added it to her already overloaded baskets.

Walking just ahead of her mom, Jenny concentrated on watching out for things on the sidewalk she might trip over. At last they made it to the pharmacy, where they were able to buy the candy they wanted. When they finally got a *trike* to stop for them, settling back into the seat felt sooooo good to Jenny. When her dad took the heavy bags from her at their gate, she felt even better. Jenny gave a huge sigh. Being home after such a big shopping trip felt wonderful.

Sunday evening, when sitting down by the tree for their family time, they discussed what to do about dividing up the things they had bought. "Angel told me," began Jenny, "that her favorite food is fried chicken, but she's only tasted it once. May we buy them a chicken?"

"Sure," Mom answered. "I can have *Ka* Tala buy one tomorrow morning. I'm planning to send her to the market for a few extra things." She paused then continued, "You know, I think I'll fry the chicken, too, before sending it over. We'll make sure Angel gets to have fried chicken."

"Then, what about the cheese balls?" Dad asked.

"We'll keep one, and I'll give the other to Tala," Mom answered. "And, by the way, I'm planning to let her leave tomorrow before lunch. She'll need time to shop and prepare for her Christmas Eve meal."

"When can we put our presents out?" Jenny asked. "And what about the ones with no names on them?"

CHRISTMAS EVE

———— ❧❦ ————

After reading together and praying, Jenny's dad asked, "Remember what you said, Jenny, about giving Angel's family the same kind of Christmas we are going to have?"

"Yes, I remember," Jenny said thoughtfully. Then her eyes lit up. "I know," she said, "God sent the matching packages for Angel and her family, didn't he?"

"Your mother and I think so," her dad answered. "Last night we unwrapped them just enough to see if they would be OK, then we wrapped them up again like they were."

"Are they OK? Can you tell me what they are?"

"The answer to the first question is 'yes,' and the answer to the second question is 'no,'" Jenny's dad said, with a twinkle in his eye. "We'll give Davy's matching ones to *Totoy* and yours to Angel. Mom's will go to Ana and her grandmother, and mine to Angel's older brother and her father."

Then, remembering what her mother had told her about gifts, Jenny asked, "Will the presents make them stop being our friends?"

"I think we can have *Ka* Tala tell them they came from a church in the States," Mom answered. "The gifts won't be from anyone they know, and they'll understand we don't want them to think they came from us."

"But they are coming from us, aren't they?" Jenny asked.

"Not really," her dad spoke up. "We didn't buy them."

"OK." Jenny didn't quite understand, but her parents seemed to feel good about it. Giving a big sigh, she added, "There is so much to learn about living in a new country."

"I feel the same way," Mom said, sighing like Jenny. "I wonder how long it will take to figure everything out."

Just then Puppy started barking wildly. Jenny's heart began beating fast. Then she heard singing. "Oh, more Christmas carolers," she said, relieved. She should have expected it by now. People had been coming almost every night for over two weeks. One group had sent a letter telling how much money they wanted toward their project when they came.

They all went outside to listen to a group of young people singing for them in English. "Please sing in *Tagalog*, too," Dad requested. They seemed pleased to sing several *Tagalog* songs. Most Filipinos sang very well. When they finished, Dad handed one of them a few coins.

Just as they sat down again, they heard more barking and singing. "Goodness, we are running out of change," Mom said, going to the desk and opening a drawer where they kept small bills and coins. "I'd like to give candy, but it's not what they want."

A group of little boys was outside the gate. Mom went out.

"I suspect the same children are coming more than once a night," Dad said, "but it's hard to tell." He got up and picked up Davy, who was nearly asleep.

"I wonder if their big brothers put them up to it," Mom said when she came back inside, "so they can buy those firecrackers."

Christmas Eve morning when *Ka* Tala was ready to take the basket of food and the presents over to Angel's house, she said, "Jenny, you can help carry."

Jenny was so excited over it all, but getting to go along... "Would it be OK?" she asked.

"I need you help me," *Ka* Tala reassured her.

As they crossed the street, Jenny saw Angel's older brother placing the family's stereo on a table in their yard. A long electric cord ran from it into the house. By the time they reached the yard, "Rudolf the Red Nosed Reindeer" was playing loudly. "We playing Christmas music for you," he said, smiling at Jenny and raising his eyebrows at *Ka* Tala.

"*Hoy*, Jun," *Ka* Tala responded. Angel stood in the doorway with *Totoy* close beside her. "*Hoy*, Angel, *Totoy*. Is Ana at your place?" she asked.

"She washing our clothes still," Angel said, not taking her eyes off the basket and bulging plastic bag. She sniffed. Jenny could smell the fried chicken in the basket, too. "Get *Ate*," Angel said to *Totoy*. He disappeared around the corner of the house as fast as his short legs could carry him.

Jenny looked past Angel into their *sala*. She did not see the *Christmas tree.*

Nanay limped around the corner from the front side of the house. "Good morning, *Nanay.* Your bones hurting today?" *Ka* Tala asked respectfully.

Before *Nanay* could answer, *Ate* Ana arrived. *Ka* Tala handed her the basket. "For you," she said. Jenny wondered what to do with the presents. Should she give all of them to *Ate,* too? Then *Ka* Tala took the plastic bag and set it on the ground. "Some little gift only," she said, looking away, "from church in the States." Then turning to *Nanay* she said, "We going now, *Nanay.*" Taking Jenny's hand, she headed back across the street.

And that was that. *How much nicer it would be,* Jenny thought, *if they would let you see how they liked things,* but she did not expect it, or a "thank you," anymore. At home, Jenny's mom was just adding the cheese ball to the basket of things they'd bought at the market for *Ka* Tala and her family. "I'm going to let you leave now, Tala," Mom said, holding out the basket. "Merry Christmas."

"Thank you, Ma'am," *Ka* Tala said, smiling at both of them as she took the heavy basket.

Turning to Jenny's mom she said, "I go now, Ma'am. Do you want I come to work again already next Wednesday, Ma'am?"

"Yes, fine. Merry Christmas," Mom said again, handing her an envelope as she left.

"So," Jenny's mom began, sitting down at the table with a pencil and paper. "Jenny, run upstairs and ask Dad to come down so we can talk over plans for

Christmas Eve and Christmas Day. He's playing with Davy in his room, I think."

Jenny ran up the stairs. Passing her bedroom door, she noticed a present sitting on her bed. Sliding to a stop on the waxed wooden floor, she backed up and went in to see what it could be. The tag on the beautifully wrapped box read, "To Jenny and David." In her parents' room, she found another package. It said, "To Ma'am and Sir."

"Look, Daddy," she said, holding out the packages as she went into David's room. "Are these from *Ka* Tala?"

"They must be," he answered, getting up from the floor. "Has *Ka* Tala left?"

"Yes. Mom wants you to come."

"OK. Davy, you go carefully down the stairs. I might as well get the rest of our presents and carry them down. It's time to put them under, well, near our tree."

Jenny was surprised to see how many presents there actually were, even though far less than they had had back home.

"Did you feel that cool breeze a minute ago?" Dad asked, sitting down at the table, then picking up David and sitting him on his lap. "The wind whistled around the windows upstairs and reminded me a little bit of Christmas weather."

"I think the first thing on our Christmas Eve day plans is hot chocolate," Mom said, getting up from the table and putting water on to heat. She set four big coffee mugs on the kitchen counter and spooned milk powder and chocolate syrup into each one. "You know what we need," she continued, "are some smaller mugs for you kids." She put the powdered milk can and jar of chocolate syrup away. "I never thought we'd be enjoying hot chocolate as much as we have lately, did you, Jenny?" she asked, when she saw Jenny's faraway look.

But Jenny wasn't thinking of their faraway home they used to have just then. "Does the wind mean we're going to have another typhoon?" she asked. "No one has come to work on Angel's roof yet. When will they come to fix it, Daddy?"

"I went by the church and asked about it again, yesterday," Dad answered. "Pastor thinks they'll do it right after Christmas."

Just then, the wind whistled around the windows again. "Is a typhoon coming?" Jenny repeated, shivering.

"No, it's just that December is a cooler time of the year, Jenny," her dad answered, "because the Philippines is in the northern hemisphere, though not nearly as far north as the United States," he added. Turning to Jenny's mom, who was now adding hot water to the cups, he asked, "Isn't it pretty close to lunch time?"

"Yes, lunch is almost ready. When I fried chicken for Angel's family, I did enough for us, and I've already cut up potatoes for fries."

"French fries?" Jenny asked. Usually they ate Filipino style—meat and vegetables in broth over rice. Jenny loved Filipino food, but French fries and fried chicken? How special!

It was a fun afternoon, too. Their parents did whatever she and her brother wanted them to do. And for supper, Mom made pizza with real pizza cheese she'd bought in Manila. The only problem was the loud music across the street. And there was no way to turn it down.

After supper, they sat together around the tree and tried to read the Christmas story from Luke. "I don't know how I can think about anything peaceful," Mom said with a sigh.

"It is hard to concentrate," Dad said, beginning over again then stopping as "Jingle Bell Rock" boomed out.

"I wonder if it will be on all night," Mom was saying when suddenly the music stopped.

"Ah," they all sighed almost at the same time. No one spoke. For a minute they just sat there quietly, enjoying the stillness.

"'Silent Night,' at last," Mom whispered.

Finally, Dad read. When he finished, Jenny asked, "Why did Angel kiss Mary and Baby Jesus in our manger scene?"

"Probably because her family does that," Dad answered.

"Why?"

"Maybe they feel that pictures are more real than we do, or that Mary is more than just a person because she was the mother of God's Son."

"Will people who think like that go to heaven when they die?" Jenny asked, remembering old *Nanay*. "I mean… Do they believe Jesus paid for their sins?"

"They believe Jesus died on the cross to pay for their sins, but I think they feel it wasn't enough to take care of everything."

"But it was, wasn't it, Daddy?"

"Remember in your Bible lessons, Jenny, you learned that God doesn't need any help?"

"I guess Angel's family doesn't know that," Jenny said thoughtfully.

CHRISTMAS AND NEW YEARS

Christmas morning was full of surprises and answered questions. Jenny now knew what was in the gifts given to Angel's family. Only the presents from *Ka* Tala were left under the tree. Jenny handed her parents' box to her mom and sat down on the floor to open the one to her and Davy.

"What could this be?" Mom asked, tipping the flat box back and forth. "What do you guess, Jenny?"

"I can't guess," Jenny answered, ripping the paper from her heavy box. Mom was taking time to remove her pretty wrapping paper without tearing it. "Be careful, Jenny," she warned. "Yours might be breakable."

"Do you know what this is, Mom?"

"Not at all," Mom answered.

Prying open the end of the box, Jenny tried to pull out what was inside. It was tight. "Will you help me, Daddy?" she asked, getting up on her knees and passing the box to her dad. He looked at her, waiting. "Please," she quickly added.

Dad pulled out two objects, each wrapped in white tissue paper. "I think one is for you, and one is for Davy," he said.

"Do you know what they are?" Jenny asked.

Before her dad could answer, she'd unwrapped the cutest little mug. It was decorated with hearts and kittens and the words, "Friends Forever."

"For our hot chocolate!" she exclaimed. "Davy is busy with his toys. May I open his, too?" she asked, going right ahead. David's mug had a picture of a black and white puppy and the word, "Cutie."

"Now, aren't those perfect," Mom said. "Davy, come see your new hot chocolate mug." He came and smiled, but went quickly back to play with his big yellow backhoe.

"Now," Mom said, handing her gift to Jenny's dad. "I've unwrapped it. Why don't you open the box? It's for both of us."

"OK," he answered. Jenny watched her dad take the lid off the box, not imagining what the gift could be. He lifted up a folded piece of cloth. When it fell open, they saw a beautifully embroidered doily.

"Just right for under this carved wooden bowl here on our coffee table," Mom exclaimed, taking it and smoothing it out. "Tala probably spent a day's pay for it. We'll need to be very careful not to spill anything on it." Mom bent to examine it more closely. "Such beautiful, detailed work," she added, running her finger over the stitching.

"*Ka* Tala sure gave us nice presents, didn't she Mom and Dad?"

"She sure did, Jenny," they answered at the same time.

After lunch, while lying on her bed for the *siesta* her parents said they all needed, Jenny thought about her presents and wondered what Angel's family thought of theirs. Was Angel really surprised when she opened her books and markers? How would *Totoy* like his set of little vehicles? If he had ever had even one truck before, Jenny didn't know it.

"What else?" she asked out loud. "Hand lotion," she answered herself. How pretty her mother's had smelled when she'd opened her bottle and shared some with her! *Ate* would love using it, especially because she had to wash so much laundry by hand. She'd like all the other stuff in the pretty gift set, too. And wouldn't *Nanay* love to feel the softness of the beautiful new towels? All towels washed and dried without machines were stiff and scratchy. Mom had said she planned to keep hers on the shelf as long as she could to enjoy the sweet smell and softness. Would *Nanay* do that, too?

"Jenny," she heard someone calling.

"What?" she answered sleepily.

"You'd better wake up now," her mom said, coming into her room. "You've slept all afternoon." Jenny hadn't even known she'd fallen asleep.

The rest of Christmas week was spent doing special things with her family and using the new markers and other things from her parents, her home church, and her grandmother. Grandma had sent more craft kits and several new outfits for Charlotte. Even though Jenny didn't actually play with Charlotte, she liked dressing her in the beautiful dresses Grandma made. Grandma promised she would teach her to sew when they went home on furlough when she was twelve.

Soon it was New Year's Eve. "At language school they warned us to close our windows as tightly as we could," Dad explained as he carried a large piece of plastic upstairs. "I'm going to tape this over that high window that doesn't shut very well."

"Will it help the firecrackers not sound so loud?" Jenny asked, already hearing plenty of explosions, even though it was barely starting to get dark.

"It's more to keep black soot from coming inside," her dad answered. "Will you hand me that roll of duct tape, Jenny? Thanks."

"What's that awful smell?" Jenny asked, holding her nose. Then remembering the same smell the night before All Saints' Day, she asked, "Are they burning tires again?"

"Kinda smells like it, doesn't it?" her dad answered. "Another reason to get our house closed up the best we can."

Jenny went into her parents' bedroom and opened a window. "There's a fire burning in front of a house up the street," she called to her dad in the other room. "And I see another one down that street across from us."

"Close the window," Dad yelled back.

During the evening, the explosions got louder and louder, and like Angel had said, it sounded like everybody in the Philippines must be setting off firecrackers. "Come here, everybody," Dad called, going to the front door. "Let's go outside on the patio a minute." Continuous flashes of different colored lights filtered through smoke so thick they could not see their neighbors' houses.

"Let's get back inside," Mom shouted above the deafening noise. She headed for the door, one hand over her mouth and nose and the other over one ear.

"Too bad you don't have three hands," Dad yelled, teasing Mom. Once they were inside with the door closed, he turned to Jenny. "I think the smells are from the fireworks, Jenny. The fires seem to be plain bonfires."

"We were told that Filipinos write their New Year's resolutions on pieces of paper and throw them in a fire," Mom added.

They got ready for bed, but Davy was the only one who fell asleep before 1:00 a.m.

Even with all they tried to do to prevent it, *Ka* Tala had lots of scrubbing to do when she came to work. All their floors were black. As Jenny rinsed the rag out for her, *Ka* Tala began talking about Fiesta. "Every city have patron saint. Whatever day in the year belong to their saint, they celebrate. Different city have different Fiesta Day. It depend on who is their saint. People say saint watch over us. I not thinking that anymore now, but old folk do, and some who not believer. Fiesta is special occasion, even for many who not Catholic," she added.

"Is Angel's family Catholic?" Jenny asked.

"Mostly they Catholic, but I think only *Nanay* go to church now. Maybe sometime Ana and Angel go. But they not believe same like us."

"*Nanay* is old," Jenny began. "If she doesn't believe Jesus paid for all her sins—"

"I know," *Ka* Tala interrupted, the corners of her mouth turning way down. "I talk to *Nanay*, and *inay* of Angel, but they not listen. I invite to our church, but they not go."

Just then Jenny heard the most awful screeching and squealing noises. She was horrified. She covered her ears. What was happening?

"Pig," *Ka* Tala said quickly. "Wait few day more and you hearing lot of pig. Everybody getting ready for Fiesta kill pig. People make so much food for all their visitor."

"Who are the visitors?" Jenny asked.

"All relative from other town. Everybody always come. We need lot of foods prepared."

"Will you kill a pig?" Jenny asked *Ka* Tala.

"Our family share pig," she answered. "I invite your family to our place," she added. "Angel's family go, too. *Nanay* not able to prepare anything to her place. You will be invited to many place," she added.

"We will?"

"Yes. You taste so much delicious foods. Fiesta is time we making *apritada* and *adobo* and *menudo*. And *buko* salad and *leche plan*. All kind of special foods. We cooking all night."

As *Ka* Tala was leaving one afternoon, she said, "I go now, Ma'am. I need three day off only. It our Fiesta. You going to our place, Ma'am?"

"You won't be coming to work for three days?" Mom asked, frowning. "I know Fiesta Day is a holiday, but… I'll have to stay home from classes, you know, if you don't come."

"Sorry, Ma'am, I will come already on Friday. I hope you go to our place," *Ka* Tala said again, smiling. "We feeling happy if you go."

"Oh, my," Jenny's mom said with a big sigh when *Ka* Tala was gone. "So many reasons not to come to work. I wonder if all missionaries have the same problems."

"Are we going to *Ka* Tala's Fiesta?" Jenny asked. "She invited us three times."

"What?" Mom asked.

Jenny wasn't sure what her mom was asking "what" for. Wasn't she listening?

"She invited us three times. Are we going to go?"

"I told her earlier we would, and we've also been invited to our Filipino teachers' homes, and our landlord's, and I think somewhere else. Our director warned us to eat tiny amounts at each place, or we'll be totally stuffed and sick before we make it all the way around."

Early the next morning, Jenny was awakened by hoarse squealing noises coming from all directions. Even though she knew what it was, the sounds were loud and horrible. She covered her ears again. Like *Ka* Tala had said, people must be killing pigs all over town. Because *Ka* Tala wasn't coming and Jenny's mom had to stay home, they'd decided to do homeschool most of the day. They wouldn't have it on Fiesta Day, and Mom wasn't sure how they might be feeling the day after Fiesta.

"For creative writing," her mother began, "I want you to write your Christmas thank-you letters. While you're doing that, I'm going to work on our prayer letter—that is if Davy will play by himself. He's still very taken up with his new backhoe and dump truck."

Jenny wrote letters to her grandma and her old Sunday School Class. She still wondered why the church had sent two of each gift. She explained what they had done with the extra gifts, telling the children about her new friend, Angel, and how poor she was, and about her mother going abroad to work.

After creative writing, Jenny's mom gave her the math assignment, and when she finished the page of problems, they had *merienda*. Then Jenny read her social studies assignment. Next, her mom introduced the new science unit and Jenny started collecting things for the project. After lunch, while Davy was taking his nap and Mom was working on their prayer letter, Jenny did her reading and spelling, and another math page. Finally, she was allowed to quit for the day.

Tomorrow, she would get to experience a Fiesta.

"Some *nipa* huts are made with bamboo walls and some are made with grass mat walls. Most of them have thatched roofs. Out in the countryside or in towns, people live in *nipa* huts or in cement or wooden houses. Filipinos plant lots of bushes and flowers by their homes and most have fences or walls around their yards. In Manila they also have big apartment buildings and condos. Which kind of home would you like best to live in?"

—Jenny

FIESTA

Fiesta Day! What would it be like? Jenny knew only one thing. There would be lots of food. She dressed and went downstairs to eat breakfast. But there wasn't any. "Mom," she called.

"Back here," her mom answered from the storage room behind the kitchen. "I'm fixing something to take to each place we visit."

"Aren't we going to eat breakfast?" Jenny asked.

"No. In a short time we'll be eating our first of many meals today."

On the way to *Ka* Tala's place, they heard a band approaching. "May we stop and watch?" Jenny asked.

Jenny's dad asked the *trike* driver to stop, then he hopped off the back of the driver's seat. While he paid for their ride, Mom eased herself out of the low-roofed sidecar, grabbing Davy's arm just in time to catch him from falling as he jumped. Then Jenny jumped down.

They stood on the side of the street with others, waiting to see the parade pass. "I didn't know they had bands and stuff here," Jenny said, looking up at her mom. On the floats, Jenny saw beautifully dressed girls of all ages, and boys wearing shear, long-sleeved shirts standing at their sides. "Look," she said, pulling on her mom's hand, "see those little girls smaller than Angel? They're wearing make-up, too."

Performers were walking along beside the parade. Each had an assistant who held out a can to collect money from the people watching. One man had a big, ugly looking snake.

"Let's get a *trike* and get going," Mom said. As they rode along, they saw shiny paper decorations strung above the streets. And people were everywhere— walking on the streets, sitting on porches, standing in doorways, and hanging out windows. Everybody seemed to be celebrating.

Jenny had been to *Ka* Tala's once with her mother. But when the *trike* pulled over and stopped, the place didn't look familiar. "We need to walk back this way, remember?" her mother said. Jenny's dad and Davy had never been there before, so they followed. Her mother led them along a dirt path between a ditch and a wall. Soon they were under some trees. The path turned this way and that, winding around bushes and fences.

Then, just as they began to hear voices, they came to a clearing and a small wooden house. Now Jenny remembered. This time she also noticed several other small wooden houses and *nipa* huts scattered around the area close to *Ka* Tala's house.

"Welcome to our place," *Ka* Tala greeted them right away as they approached her open doorway. "Come in." Inside, chairs lined the walls of the *sala*. Filipino people occupied most of them. When Jenny and her family came in the door, everyone stopped talking and watched them.

"Please, sit down," *Ka* Tala said, smiling. People started asking her parents if they were from the States and the other usual questions.

Jenny looked through a wide doorway and saw a long table loaded with food. Ladies were clearing away partly empty dishes and adding new full ones. In a minute, *Ka* Tala brought each of them a clean plate and a spoon and fork. "Come, you get food now," she invited. The table and the food looked like no one else had taken anything yet, though Jenny had seen others eating. *Ka* Tala went along with them and named the different mixtures. "This one we make with goat meat. It taste good," she said, smiling and putting a small spoonful on Jenny's rice. Without being able to help it, the tiny servings she was supposed to take filled up her whole plate.

Just as she turned to go back to her seat in the *sala*, she saw Angel and *Nanay* sitting on chairs around the corner. "May I sit by them, Mom?" she asked, noticing Angel moving over to the edge of her chair, trying to make room for her.

"OK," was all her mom said. She was plenty busy with her own plate and looking after David, who was clinging to her legs. People were making a big fuss over him, trying to give him bites of food from their plates. Jenny's dad was heading out to the porch where many of the men had gathered.

"*Ka* Tala told me you were coming, Angel," Jenny said, sitting down on the chair where *Nanay* had been. "Where is *Nanay* going?" she asked, afraid she was taking away the old woman's place to sit.

"To kitchen. She helping *Ate* Tala. Next time my *inay* make Fiesta to our place," Angel added.

"Oh, guess what, Angel? I forgot to tell you. Our mothers used to know each other!"

Angel's eyes opened wide and she covered her open mouth with her small hand. "For sure?" she whispered.

"When your mama worked in Manila in the missionary kids' school dorm—when *Ate* was a baby— my mom was one of the girls there. She remembers your mama."

"For sure?" Angel repeated, her eyebrows rising.

"For sure," Jenny said, looking down at the plate on her lap and trying to remember which part was the goat meat. She might not try everything, she thought. So many different things, what was in them? She took a bite. It tasted good. Then she felt Angel's hand patting her arm.

"I planning to buy little Christmas present for you, but the money not come to us. *Tiya* Nene say she have big problem now. She take money for her need. We not get any. It so hard for us," she ended, the corners of her mouth turning down in the most pitiful expression.

"I'm sorry," was all Jenny could think of to say. She did not understand how such awful things always happened. "Are you going to eat?" she asked, noticing Angel didn't have a plate.

"I eat already," she answered.

Jenny forgot she was only to eat a little. She enjoyed bites of all the different things except for the one that tasted like liver. She could not remember which one was goat meat. Her favorite was the rich custard with caramel sauce they called *leche plan*. She would have liked more than the tiny sliver *Ka* Tala put on her plate.

Jenny began to notice Angel smiling at someone. She looked up and saw her mom coming toward them with Davy hanging onto her skirt and trying to hide his face. People were still holding out little spoonsful of food to him. "It's time to go now," Mom said, reaching down and taking Jenny's plate.

"Go now," Davy echoed.

"I wish I could stay here with you," Jenny told Angel as she stood up. "Maybe tomorrow we can play."

Angel nodded her head and smiled. "Bye, Ma'am," she said, looking up at Jenny's mom.

Once back out on the street, they signaled a *trike* and rode to one of her parents' teacher's house. The very same thing was going on. They went in and sat down with many others. Ladies fixed up the table with new dishes of food, and then brought them their plates and silverware. "The only thing I can eat is *leche plan*," Jenny whispered to her mother, who frowned at her.

Each time they got out of a *trike,* as they went from place to place, beggars were nearby asking for money. Young women with their heads covered in kerchiefs and carrying a small child, ragged-looking men, even children with pitiful expressions on their dirty faces held out their little hands to them. Jenny had seen beggars in Manila when they first arrived in the Philippines, and there were always a few around the market, but never as many as on this Fiesta Day.

At each place they visited, Jenny's parents took a little, but she couldn't touch one more bite. Sometimes they met other missionaries from the language school. None of them had children Jenny's age, so she hardly knew them. Whenever the missionaries got together for fellowship meetings or games, she ended up just playing with David while her parents visited.

"I don't think I can go to any more places," Mom said to Dad when they left the fourth house. She pressed one hand against her stomach. The look on her mom's face reminded Jenny of the pitiful expression the beggars made when they were begging.

"Maybe if we walk to the next place, it would help," Dad answered. "We are not going to be able to skip anybody."

"There just is a limit," Mom answered abruptly. "I mean it. I can't. I'm going to be sick."

"Well," Dad said, putting his hand up and rubbing his chin. "Why don't I get you a *trike,* and you can take the children home. I'll tell them the kids were getting too tired."

"Which is the truth," Mom answered, looking at their pained faces. "You have both done very well, though," she said to Jenny and David. "I'm proud of you."

Jenny was really glad to go home. She had a terrible stomachache and did not complain at all when her mother told her to go up and lie on her bed.

After suppertime had passed with no one even mentioning it, Jenny's dad said, "I'd like to go into town to see the procession for the patron saint."

"May I go, too? Please," Jenny begged.

"Well," Dad said slowly, turning to Jenny's mom. "What do you think about her going?"

"She's been asking questions about what Filipinos believe," Mom answered. "I guess it's OK."

EASTER AND
FLORES de MAYO

In the darkness, Jenny climbed out of the *trike* near the plaza in front of the big church in town. As her dad paid the driver, she began watching a group of people carrying candles. High on a flower-decorated cart, a stiff statue of a person bobbed along with them. In the flickering candlelight, Jenny saw hands reaching up to pat the statue and ladies rubbing it with small pieces of cloth. Was that old woman who was limping Angel's *nanay*?

Jenny didn't say anything while they stood with others in the darkness, watching the procession move slowly along the street around the plaza. And she didn't say anything when she and her dad got in another *trike,* or as they rode home past dimly lit houses and small booths where people were cooking over charcoal fires. But as soon as they were back inside her house, she asked, "Were those people worshipping an idol, Daddy?"

"I don't know," he answered, thoughtfully. "I don't know what they are really thinking."

Jenny went quietly upstairs to get ready for bed. When her dad came to pray with her, she could only think of what she had just seen. "Please, God," she prayed. "Help those old people to believe you already paid for all their sins before they die."

The next morning, neither of Jenny's parents felt up to going to class, so it was just as well that *Ka* Tala wasn't coming. They spent most of the day lying around with stomachaches. "Oh," Mom moaned, heading for the bathroom again. "What did we eat at Fiesta that did this to us? Everything tasted so good."

"I thought everything tasted good, too," Jenny's dad said, getting up and heading for the other bathroom. "I guess we just ate too much."

Next, it was Jenny's turn in the bathroom. And so the day passed.

By the following morning, they were doing better, except for David. "I think I'd better stay home, even though *Ka* Tala is here," Mom said to Jenny's dad, as she sat down at the table next to David's high chair. "I can't leave with him feeling this way. We'll give him lots of fluids, and hopefully I can get back to class on Monday."

"OK," Jenny's dad said. "I'm late. Hope a *trike* comes along right away." He gave Mom a quick kiss then hurried out the door with his language book. "I'll see you around noon," he called back as he unlatched the gate. "Sure hope Davy's feeling a lot better by then."

"Many sick after Fiesta, Ma'am," said *Ka* Tala, who was washing dishes. "Even Filipino. 'Cuz people cooking foods early and it sitting all day and all night. They not have fridge."

"Oh," Mom replied, as she helped Davy with his drink of Jell-O water.

"Mom," Jenny said, when she sat down at the table to have juice and crackers. "Know what Angel told me at Fiesta? More money came from her mother, but this time her aunt took it. They didn't get any again. Do you think that's fair, Mom?" she asked.

Ka Tala turned from the sink and came over to the table. "Angel's mother fix now, Ma'am," she said. "Only one who get money from bank is *Nanay*. Jo Jo—father of Angel—tell my sister-in-law they planning to start sewing business when Angel's mother come home. It important saving the money. *Nanay* get only for their family need. Bank not allow Romy or Nene taking any more next time."

"Good," Jenny and her mom said at the same time.

Christmas cards from friends and family back home arrived throughout the month of January. "Look what it cost people to send these," Mom commented. "It was sure thoughtful of them. I'll save them, too, for next year, so we'll have cards to look at during Christmas."

In the card from Pastor and his wife, they found out how they'd happened to receive double gifts. "I don't know what you are needing them for," Pastor's wife wrote, "but by mistake your names and gift lists were given out to two Sunday school classes. When the gifts came in, the people felt God must have had a reason for it. So rather than taking them back, they went out and bought more gifts for the missionary family whose names were missed."

"Now they know why God allowed that," Mom said. "They should have received our letters by now. At least, I think the Christmas mail tie-up is past."

Toward the end of January, men came and repaired Angel's roof. Then for the next couple of months things went along pretty routinely. *Ka* Tala came Monday through Friday, and Mom and Dad went to classes in the mornings. While her parents were gone, Jenny entertained herself or played with her brother or with Angel. In the afternoons, Jenny and her mom continued to work on her third-grade homeschool lessons. At the end of March, *Ate* Ana graduated from high school and came back to work part-time.

Then one afternoon in early April, while working on a story she was writing for extra credit, Jenny wandered over to the window. Looking out, she saw something strange. Coming down the middle of the street was a small group of people. In the lead was a person carrying a large wooden cross over his shoulder. All the people were walking barefooted. "*Ka* Tala," Jenny called, running to get her to come look. "What is that?" she asked, pointing out the window.

"It Holy Week. They do that so they suffering like Jesus," *Ka* Tala explained. "See, they trying to step on rock."

"What?" Jenny asked, confused. She looked outside again and saw that they were all walking on the worst parts of the street. A few lagging behind the others were limping.

"They want God know they sorry Jesus suffer. Some Catholic say if they suffer, God accept them."

During Easter week, Jenny found out more about what many Filipinos believe. She learned that Good Friday is the most important day, because it's the day that Jesus died. Only sad, slow music played over the radio.

Saturday morning when they woke up, they did not hear one sound. No *trikes* going by. No voices of children playing outside. No dogs barking or roosters crowing. Never before had it been so quiet since their coming to the Philippines. "Some Filipinos believe God is dead today," Dad told Jenny, as the family ate their breakfast. "They are afraid to go anywhere, because they think God is not able to take care of them today."

"What are we going to do?" Jenny asked.

"About what?" Dad asked her.

"About them," Jenny answered.

"We did come over here to teach Filipinos about God," Mom said.

"But why aren't we doing it?"

"In order to do it, we need to learn the language first," her dad explained. "They have advised us not to teach any Bible classes while we are in language study this year."

"But why?" Jenny asked, frowning.

"Because, if we spend too much time preparing Bible studies, we won't have the time we need to learn the language. But after we finish, we'll be doing all kinds of teaching," her dad answered.

"Remember the club we used to have at Grandma's house, Mom?" Jenny asked.

"The Bible Club?"

"Yes. We can have a Bible Club. You wouldn't need to prepare. *Ka* Tala could teach."

"It would still be a lot of work for your mother," Dad said.

"Please, Mom," Jenny begged.

"I suppose when we're done with your homeschooling—"

"I don't think you should," Jenny's dad interrupted.

"Well, let's not talk about it anymore now," Mom said, getting up and beginning to clear the table.

By evening, people were moving around again, and on Easter Sunday everything was back to the same usual noisy activities. At church, the believers celebrated the resurrection, but for everyone else, the day was a regular Sunday.

In the late afternoon on the last Friday in April, Jenny and her family began hearing music over a loudspeaker. All evening men and women talked, announced games for children, and had singing contests. The sound was so loud Jenny's family could easily hear every word, even with the windows closed. The same thing happened on Saturday and again on Sunday. "Oh, my," Mom said, sighing. "What celebration is this?"

It was not long before they found out—Mom and Dad at language school and Jenny from *Ka* Tala and *Ate* Ana. The name of the celebration was *Flores de Mayo*.

"We make pretty place for our Virgin Mary," Angel said one day, excitedly showing Jenny a corner in their *sala* where they had a small statue of Mary. "We light candle. We pray. Every day we put more flower. Every night they having party. *Kuya* go. *Ate* go sometime. Mary happy we making good time to her. She pray for us."

That afternoon during homeschool, when Jenny was asked to write a story about a Filipino celebration, she said, "Mom, we need to have a Bible Club. Angel worships Mary. She doesn't know anything about the Bible."

"When we finish your third-grade requirements, we'll discuss it," was all Mom said.

After her mom had gone downstairs to work with *Ate* Ana on supper, Jenny decided to see what *Ka* Tala might say about it. *Maybe she shouldn't ask, but what was going to happen to Angel's family?* She went into her parents' room, where *Ka* Tala was waxing the wood floor. "*Ka* Tala, at my grandma's in the States we used to have a Bible Club. We learned songs and verses and had Bible stories. Lots of children came."

"I know Bible Club," *Ka* Tala said, rising up on her knees and pushing her hair away from her eyes with the back of her hand. "Last time I work to missionary, I helping teach Bible Club."

"You did?" Jenny couldn't believe her ears. "You mean you know how already?"

"I teach everything. Missionary not know yet how to speak *Tagalog*."

Not waiting for more explanation, Jenny flew down the stairs. "Mom, *Ka* Tala already knows how to teach a Bible Club. She did it for another missionary before. She—"

"Slow down," Mom said, turning around from the sink. "We'll talk to Dad, then if we decide to try it, I'll talk with her more. But you heard what Dad said before."

Jenny had to be satisfied with that. She couldn't wait for her dad to come home, so she could tell him about it. But when her dad came home for supper, after going out to practice his *Tagalog*, his face looked like he, too, had something exciting to share with the family.

ANGEL'S FAMILY

Jenny knew she was not allowed to bring up family discussions while the house girls were there. And Dad didn't mention his surprise at supper either. After *Ate* Ana finished the dishes, she had ironing to do, so she didn't leave until almost time for Jenny to get ready for bed. *House girls are a big help,* Jenny thought, *but sometimes they are here just too long.* Anyway, she didn't know why they couldn't talk about things when they were around.

As soon as *Ate* left, Mom came up to Jenny's bedroom where Dad had been waiting since getting Davy to sleep. Mom sat down on the bed, too.

"I had a long talk with Jo Jo this afternoon," Dad began.

"*Ate* and Angel's father?" Jenny asked.

"Yes. He gave me a ride when I went into town after lunch. I asked him a couple questions, and he just kept talking. It seems that when he was a boy, his mother took him to a Bible-believing church. He said he accepted Jesus as his Savior when he was about ten years old."

"Oh, Daddy. You mean... but..." Jenny could not get her words out.

"He said when he was a teenager," Jenny's dad continued, "he gradually stopped going to church. Then he married Angel's mother who was Catholic. He went to church with her for a while, but he soon quit going because he didn't believe what they taught."

"Why didn't he—?"

"Jenny, wait, let me tell you the rest," Dad said. "When they were married, they moved in with his wife's family."

"With *Nanay*?" Jenny asked.

"Yes, but not across the street where they are now. They lived in a barrio farther out of town. They had Jun and Ana and a new baby boy, when his wife decided to go abroad to work."

"You mean Angel's mother worked abroad before now?"

"Yes, Jenny, but Angel wasn't born yet. Ana was only about *Totoy*'s age. Jo Jo decided to give the baby boy to his mother, Angel's other grandmother, to raise because she was lonely, and because his wife would not be home for two years."

"Oh, my," Mom said.

"Then," Dad continued, "when his wife came home, the grandmother had become so attached to the boy she couldn't give him back."

"Oh, dear!" Mom said with a big sigh.

"Not finished yet," Dad said. "After a year at home, Angel's mother decided to go abroad again, but now she had another new baby boy."

"Did they give him away, too?" Jenny asked.

"Jo Jo's mother begged for him. She said the other little boy needed a playmate, so Jo Jo let her take him,"

Dad went on. "His wife would be gone again for two more years."

"They didn't get that boy back, either." Jenny said. "Now I know what Angel meant. A long time ago when I was at *Totoy*'s birthday party, Angel said she thought she had two more brothers, but she wasn't sure."

"Anyway," Dad continued, "when his wife came back, they bought this place across the street and moved out of the family barrio in order to have a home of their own. He said his wife's brother and sister never liked it that they moved."

"That's Angel's *Tiyo* Romy and *Tiya* Nene," Jenny explained. "I knew *Tiya* Nene and Angel's mother didn't get along, but I didn't know that's why."

"Maybe a little jealousy there, too," Mom guessed. "Did *Nanay* come with them?"

"Not right away. She came later when there was trouble between family members in the barrio," Dad answered. "And also, I think to help with the new baby."

"The new baby was Angel," Jenny said, smiling. "I'm glad they got to keep her. But what about their other boys who never lived with them?"

"I guess they're about eleven and fourteen years old. Jo Jo says they still go to church with his mother. He hopes they won't quit like he did. But he is worried about them, because his mother is getting quite old and can't always know what they're doing."

"Oh, my," was all Mom could say.

"He's concerned about his other children, too," Dad continued. "He'd like for them to go to a good church, but he doesn't seem to know what to do about it."

"Our Bible Club!" Jenny exclaimed, sitting straight up in bed. "Daddy, I found out that *Ka* Tala taught a Bible Club before, when she was working for another missionary. She could teach our club, and it wouldn't take Mom's time."

"Really?" he said, looking at Jenny's mother.

"That's what she told Jenny. I haven't talked with her about it," Mom answered.

"What do you think about doing it?" Dad asked her.

"Well, by the end of this week I'll be finished with Jenny's homeschooling."

"Why don't you think it through and talk with Tala? Just see what it would involve," Dad suggested. "Then we'll make a decision."

"Oh, thank you, Daddy," Jenny said, getting up on her knees and giving her father a hug.

Jenny was so excited she could hardly get to sleep. She kept thinking over and over how they could start the Bible Club. They could ask *Ate* Ana to help, so she would hear the Bible lessons, too, even though she was too old to be in the club. And Angel could help invite the children in the neighborhood. What about *Totoy*? He was too little, she decided. And what about the two brothers that Angel didn't even know for sure were her brothers? And where would they have the Bible Club?

Jenny woke up late the next morning, but just before *Ka* Tala arrived, she asked her parents if she could talk to her about the Bible Club.

"No," her dad answered. "Mom needs to do that, but first she needs to think about it."

"Actually, I stayed up and thought about it some last night," Mom said. "I would like to discuss it with you, too, Jenny. Maybe you and I can talk it over later this afternoon when you've finished your schoolwork for the day. Then we'll mention it to *Ka* Tala before she goes home."

"May I tell Angel?" Jenny called from the door, as her parents were on their way out the gate to catch a *trike* to go to the language school.

"No," was the answer again.

"Oh, why do grown-ups have to do so much thinking before they start anything?" she muttered as she started up the stairs to do her chores. While making her bed and straightening her room, she thought and thought and thought about what they might do for Bible Club.

That afternoon, while she was writing sentences for her new spelling words, Jenny heard thumps and bumps in her parents' room. "What is going on?" she asked herself out loud. Getting up and heading into the room, she saw her mom kneeling by a large box on the floor.

"What's that stuff?" Jenny asked, not recognizing the box.

"This was left behind by missionaries who were at the language school last year. They gave it to us when we first came. I'd forgotten about it. It's Bible stories and pictures."

Jenny reached in the box and took out a large envelope of something. "What's in here?" she asked.

"I don't know. You may look," her mom said, already busy reading through a large picture storybook she'd just found.

Jenny tore open the envelope and dumped out all kinds of trinkets. "Are these prizes?" she asked.

"Could be," Mom answered. "Please put them back in the envelope for now. Have you finished your spelling?"

"No," Jenny said. She picked up the plastic toys and stuffed them back in the torn envelope. "I'll be so glad when this week is over. Schoolwork takes so long," she said, looking at her watch.

"What time is it?" Mom asked, as she picked up a spiral notebook from the box. "We'll probably have to wait until tomorrow to talk to *Ka* Tala. This looks like plans all written out for Bible Club meetings," she said, flipping through the pages. "Go finish your spelling, Jenny. What time is it?"

"Four thirty-seven," Jenny answered, as she got up and slowly returned to her room. She heard her mom go downstairs. Before sitting down at her desk, she went to her window to see what the children whose voices she heard below were doing. She saw them picking flowers from branches of her mother's bushes that had grown long enough to hang down over the outside of their wall. "For Mary," Jenny said. And she knew it would be another noisy night.

Loud music and talking were still going on when Jenny's mother told her to get ready for bed. "I'll be up in a minute, and we'll talk about Bible Club a bit before you go to sleep. If anybody can go to sleep," she added.

A few minutes later, her mom came in and sat down on the bed. "That guy on the loudspeaker, now, sounds like he keeps dropping off to sleep. He must be drunk."

"Did you know they're getting flowers from our bushes for their *Mary places*?" Jenny asked her mother.

"How? Oh, you mean from the ones hanging over the wall? Well, I guess anything outside the wall is pretty much up for grabs," her mom answered. "Now, one thing first. You realize, don't you, Jenny, that we'll only be here one more month?"

"What do you mean?" Jenny asked, alarmed. They hadn't even started telling people about Jesus yet. "Are we going back to the States already? I thought I'd be twelve years old when—"

"No, not back there," her mom interrupted. "We're only here in this town for our year of studying the national language. Did you forget that, Jenny? When we're finished with the course, we'll be moving to another location."

"Not me," Jenny said, scowling fiercely. "I'm not moving!"

PLANS

Jenny couldn't imagine worse news than what her mother had just told her. She stared at the spot on the ceiling above her bed. Why should they move? How could they move, just when they were going to start a Bible Club? All year they'd worked hard to get used to living here. Now when it finally felt like home, they had to move away? For certain, she could not move, Jenny concluded. She kept staring at the spot on the ceiling.

"Jenny," she heard her mother say. She didn't answer.

"Would you like to talk about the Bible Club now?" her mother asked. "Or do you want to wait until tomorrow?"

"I'll go live with Angel, if you want to move so much," Jenny said, turning over to face the wall.

"I'm sorry this has upset you, Jenny," her mother said softly. "We should have talked about it all along, so you would have been more prepared. We have to be out of this house by a certain date. Another family is planning to rent this place when they come for their year of language study. We can still start the Bible Club before we leave. We have a month."

Jenny said nothing. She was frustrated and heartbroken and worn out.

"I'm going to pray, and we'll talk again tomorrow," her mom said. After asking God to encourage Jenny and work everything out according to his will, she bent and kissed her lightly on the cheek. "I love you," she whispered.

Jenny said nothing. After her mother turned out the light and went downstairs, Jenny cried quietly. "How can this awful thing be happening?" she whispered to God. "I know you want Angel and her family and the other people to hear the truth before they die. And I don't want to have to leave my friends and my home again. Everything is so hard."

Jenny began thinking about hard things. Angel's mother and father had given away two of their babies and couldn't get them back. Angel's mother had to be gone for more than a year, even though *Totoy* was only two years old. Angel couldn't go to school because there was no money. They depended on Mary to pray for them. *Nanay* believed an idol could help her. They didn't know that Jesus had paid for all of their sin, and that they didn't have to walk on rocks with bare feet to make God accept them.

The Bible Club was important. God would want them to have it; she was sure. So God would work it out. What had Mom prayed? "That God would work everything out according to his will." Yes, God would do that.

She must have been thinking for a long time, because she heard her parents coming up the stairs to go to bed. "Mom," Jenny called. Her mother stopped at the door. "Mom, I'm sorry for what I said."

"I forgive you, Dear," Mom answered, walking to Jenny's bed and sitting down. Jenny reached up in the dim light to hug her. "It's not easy, I know," her mother said, bending over and holding her gently. "God has helped your dad and me so much this year, and I know he's worked in your heart, too. I believe he has more good things for us before we move."

"I do, too," Jenny said, snuggling down in her comfortable bed.

The next day, while Angel was over playing with Jenny, they planned how to start the Bible Club, using the things in the spiral notebook Mom had found. "I want to get the girls who do Christian Ed. at church to work with you, Tala," Jenny's mom said after *Ka* Tala agreed to teach. "That way it will be a church outreach and won't come to an end when we leave."

Jenny's job would be to cut and fold invitations that Mom would make on the computer. Angel could help. *Ate* Ana was to be in charge of *merienda*. Jenny's mom asked *Ka* Tala to stop at the church on her way home and ask the Christian Ed. director to come by to talk about the Bible Club.

Just before Angel left, she told Jenny, "I tell *Tatay* we having club. He be happy for club. Maybe our brother attending, too."

"You mean *Totoy*?"

"Maybe he come. Other brother. One not live to our place."

"You mean the brothers who live with your other grandmother?"

"Yes. I tell *Ate* she invite, most especially Bobby. He not too old for our club."

"We will be glad for him to come," Jenny said, opening the gate for Angel.

A couple days later, just after *Ate* Ana brought Davy down from his nap, Jenny heard her mom call out from the room where she studied. "Please give Davy a drink and one cookie, Jenny. I have to do my lesson for tomorrow, and I need to have Ana prepare vegetables for supper."

"Last time *Ate* Tala bring me to Bible Club she teaching," *Ate* Ana said, handing Jenny the pitcher of juice as she looked for the vegetables. "I really like, but I only able to attend three time. I like I can help to our club."

"We might have the first one on my birthday," Jenny said, pouring Davy a drink.

"Angel's birthday soon. But we not able having party this time." *Ate* Ana frowned sadly.

"She can have her party with me," Jenny exclaimed then quickly added, "but I have to ask my mother first."

"Jenny," her mother called from the other room. "Come here, please."

Jenny knew her mother had not yet agreed to have the Bible Club on her birthday. "I didn't say we'd celebrate while the children are here," Jenny said as soon as she reached the door.

"Come in and shut the door," Mom commanded. "Do you remember what we said about having the club on your birthday?"

"Yes."

"What was it?"

"Seeing the children listening to a Bible story for the first time would be a better present than having a party," Jenny answered.

"And the idea was that they would not know it was your birthday. Now you've told Ana. That was not right."

"Sorry, Mom."

"We'll have to see about the date of the Bible Club. You'll probably not get to have it on your birthday. It would have been a very special birthday present for you."

"But, can't we have only *Ate* and Angel share the secret with me?"

"I don't think that will work. Tell Ana that neither the club date nor your birthday celebration has been planned yet. And don't tell her the date of your birthday."

Jenny opened the door and started up the stairs toward her room.

"Come back and play with Davy," Mom called. Just then they heard barking and a call from outside the gate. *Ate* Ana went out and returned with the Christian Ed. ladies.

Jenny took David outside and played with Puppy. Puppy was no longer a puppy, but she was a nice pet and had learned several tricks, as well as being a good watchdog.

"Mom," Jenny said later at supper. "What will we do with Puppy when the children come for Bible Club?"

"I suppose we'll tie her at the back of the yard, or else put her inside in the back room."

"What is the date for the first club?" Jenny's dad asked.

Jenny had wanted to ask, but hesitated to bring it up because of the problem earlier. "Can we still have it on my birthday?" she pleaded.

"I feel it would complicate the true purpose of the club, Jenny, especially now that someone knows about your birthday," Mom answered. "Also, now that you know about Angel's birthday and have invited her to share yours."

"I said I'd have to ask first," Jenny reminded her mom.

"Well, I think the invitation has already been given by what you said. And we couldn't go back on that now. Anyway we'd be happy to have Angel celebrate her birthday with us. When is it exactly?"

"I don't know, but I'll ask *Ate* tomorrow."

"Also," Mom continued, "we can't have the club next week, because the girls from church have other things to do and prefer to wait until the following week."

"Oh, Mom, we'll only have time for two or three clubs before we leave. Why do we—?"

"That reminds me," her dad interrupted. "We didn't tell you yet that we had a message from our office in Manila. The family coming to rent this house has been delayed a month. We'll be staying here until it's time to take you to school."

"School?" Jenny asked, missing the good news about staying an extra month.

"I guess we haven't talked about that in a long time either," Mom said, sighing.

"You mean MK school?" Jenny asked. At the field conference she'd heard boys and girls talking about the missionary kids' school they attended. They'd told about lots of fun times, but when Jenny heard that the kids stayed there without their parents, she was not so sure. *What would she do if…?*

"We think the MK school will be a great place for you to be, Jenny," Dad continued.

"But I didn't know—"

"It's OK," Mom interrupted. "We still have time to talk about it together and give you a chance to…"

Jenny's mom suddenly got up from the table and left the room. Jenny looked at her dad. "What's wrong with Mom?" she asked.

"The little white flowers painted on this mirror are the Philippine national flower–*sampaguita*. You should smell them! They are really sweet. People make necklaces with them and sell them to travelers."

—Jenny

BIRTHDAY PARTY

"Mom feels a lot like you do right now, Jenny, thinking about you being separated from us. It will not be easy," Jenny's dad went on, "but we've been praying about it for some time. And remember last year, Jenny, how much you wanted to go to a real school?"

"But I don't have to go to a real school," Jenny said quickly. "I can homeschool again."

"It will be good for you to have American friends again, though we hope you'll make more Filipino friends, too," Dad added.

"But what about Davy?" Jenny asked.

"Right now it's time for Davy to get ready for bed," Mom said, coming back to the table and picking him up. "We won't make you go, Jenny. We'll talk about it more soon."

The next day when *Ate* Ana arrived, she brought a flower, which she placed in a glass of water and set on the table. "Angel send. She know you like," *Ate* explained. "*Nanay* have orchid plant. It making flower."

"Angel sent this to me?" Jenny asked, never having seen an orchid before, but knowing it was really special. "Tell her... well... I do like it... a lot," she said, then she asked, "*Ate*, when is Angel's birthday?"

"Next May twenty already," she answered.

"May twentieth?" Jenny couldn't believe it. "You mean next Wednesday is Angel's birthday?" She almost said, "too." Could it really be possible? Nobody would believe it!

"You have surprise for Angel?" *Ate* Ana asked, looking at the excitement in Jenny's eyes.

"Yes. Yes, I have a very big surprise." She wasn't supposed to tell her birthday, but she couldn't hold it back. "May twentieth is my birthday, too, *Ate!*"

"For sure?" *Ate* Ana said raising her eyebrows and opening her mouth.

Less than a week later Jenny found herself excitedly waiting at their gate. David's third birthday had passed several weeks ago with only a family celebration, but for her birthday, Angel and *Ate* Ana would join them. In fact, the party was for Angel, too. Nobody could get over finding out that she and Angel shared the exact same birthday. Mom said she'd plan their whole party, if that was OK with Jenny, so it would be a surprise for both of them. Jenny had no idea what they would be doing in just a very few minutes.

Then Angel arrived. She was wearing a pretty new pink dress. "Your dress is beautiful," Jenny greeted her, as she opened the gate and drew Angel inside.

"Oh, this not so pretty like your dress," she answered. "Our good news is we happy 'cuz *Inay* send message. She say now the time right we start building new room to our place."

"Is your mother coming home soon?" Jenny asked, feeling very happy for Angel.

"Yes, she come next Christmas, or if not, she come to Fiesta," Angel answered, smiling.

Jenny frowned. "I thought she was just staying one year." She remembered Angel's mother leaving in early November, right after All Saints' Day.

"Yes. She stay little longer only 'cuz money not enough," Angel continued. "Anyway we start construction. When she come, sewing room ready. *Inay* will buy sewing machine."

"Happy Birthday, Angel!" Mom said, coming out the door, followed by *Ate* Ana carrying David. "Are you girls ready for your party? Dad will be here to get us in a minute."

Jenny forgot about Angel's mother's delay in coming, because just then a car turned the corner and stopped outside their gate. Jenny didn't believe her eyes when she saw that the driver was her father. She had become so used to not riding in a car, she'd almost forgotten about cars. She looked at Angel. Angel's eyes were big.

"Whose car is it? Where are we going?" Jenny asked her mom.

"You'll see," Mom answered, climbing into the front seat and taking Davy from *Ate*.

"I borrowed the car from one of the missionaries at the language school," her dad answered her first question. "You may get in now, girls," he said, holding the driver's seat forward, so they could climb into the back. *Ate* Ana, who was seated in the middle, reached out and took Jenny and Angel's hands and held them tightly. Neither sister said a word.

It wasn't long until Jenny spotted something ahead that she'd never expected to see way out here in the province. She remembered her surprise in finding a McDonald's in Manila the first day they'd arrived in the Philippines. "McDonald's? Right here where we live?" she asked.

"It just opened this week," Dad said. "Your mom and I decided not to tell you, but to make it a birthday treat."

Jenny looked at Angel and *Ate* Ana. They still hadn't spoken. "Have you been to McDonald's before?" she asked.

"This our first time," *Ate* answered almost in a whisper.

Jenny's dad parked the car and they went inside, through a door held open for them by a smiling uniformed guard with a gun strapped over his shoulder.

"You may order whatever you like," Mom said to the girls, as she read out different things listed on the menu. *Ate* ordered spaghetti. Angel started to say "spaghetti," but her eyes were looking at the picture of a big piece of chicken.

"Would you like the fried chicken?" Mom asked her.

"She like," *Ate* Ana spoke up.

Jenny ordered a hamburger and fries. Then, looking up at the menu, she spotted a picture of a big, thick, pink shake. She could already taste it. Smiling excitedly she asked, "Mom, may we order strawberry shakes? I know *Ate* and Angel would love strawberry, too."

"OK," Mom answered, giving the order to the girl behind the counter.

"Vanilla our flavor of the week," the girl said, smiling at the three girls. "You like three vanilla milkshake?"

Jenny's smile faded.

"We'll all take Sprite, I think," Mom said. As they waited for their food she told the girls, "I have cake at home. They aren't set up here yet to do birthdays."

Jenny enjoyed her treat very much and it was fun to watch Angel and *Ate* Ana eating at McDonald's for their first time.

On the way home the girls were again very quiet. "Are you having a happy birthday?" Jenny asked Angel who was sitting next to her this time.

"Yes," she answered, smiling.

"First time Angel riding in car," *Ate* said.

"Oh," Jenny said. She had not thought of that. "But you've ridden in one before," she said, turning to *Ate* Ana.

"Yes, one time, I think," she answered hesitantly.

When they walked into the house, Jenny saw their table set with party plates and cups and napkins. In the middle were two decorated cakes. One said, "Happy Birthday, Jenny" and the other, "Happy Birthday, Angel." On each cake were nine candles.

After they sang and prayed and blew out the candles, Mom put a small piece of each cake on their plates. One turned out to be chocolate and the other white. Dad came from the kitchen with a tub of something from the tiny freezer in their fridge. "Can anybody eat a scoop of this old strawberry ice cream?" he asked, laughing.

"Strawberry?" Jenny exclaimed, smiling at her dad. This was the best birthday party she'd ever had!

After eating their cake and ice cream, Mom brought out the gifts. Jenny wondered what Angel would do. She whispered to Angel, "You don't have to open them now." But Angel was already taking the ribbon off the yellow box. Jenny picked up her yellow box. In the boxes were matching necklace and earring sets. "Thank you, Mom and Dad," Jenny said when she saw them.

"Thank you, Ma'am and Sir," Angel said quietly, smiling shyly.

Next they opened the pink boxes. In them were identical T-shirts, except Angel's was smaller. One more gift was left for each of the girls. But these were not matching. Jenny knew what was in Angel's, but hers was a mystery. What could it be? She let Angel open hers first. Angel gasped when she drew a large object from the box. Jenny hoped Angel would like the backpack she and her mother had picked out at the market.

"It for when I going to school. *Nanay* buy uniform and shoe, but money not enough for bag," she said, looking down at the backpack and smiling broadly.

"Thank you, Ma'am," *Ate* Ana said this time, running her hand over the backpack. "It so nice Angel having new book bag for school."

Jenny thought how fun it was to give things to her new friends. "Oh," she said, noticing her unopened gift. "Shall I open my last one?" She pulled off the bow and ribbon, peeled up the tape, and unfolded the wrapping-paper flap on the top. Inside the box under the tissue paper was a hand painted brush, comb and mirror set.

"I love it," Jenny said, carefully lifting them out of the box. "Thank you so much, *Ate* and Angel," she said, meaning it with all her heart.

"May I see them, Jenny?" Mom asked. "They're beautiful. Are these small white flowers *sampaguita*?" she asked, looking over at *Ate* Ana.

"Yes. Our Philippine flower."

After the girls left, Mom said, "Now I know why the money was not enough for the backpack." She held up the mirror and looked again at the delicately painted flowers.

"The set is very special, isn't it, Mom?"

"It is very special, Jenny, especially because of who it's from."

"Before I forget," Dad spoke up, "you'll both be glad to hear that since we'll be staying an extra month after we finish language school, I've made arrangements to have a Bible study with Angel's father."

"Great," Jenny said, reaching both arms around her dad and giving him a big hug. "And next week's our first Bible Club, so Angel and *Ate* will start to learn about Jesus, too."

BIBLE CLUB

Jenny and Angel and *Ate* Ana walked from house to house, passing out invitations to the Bible Club. "That's really a nice place," Jenny said after leaving one beautifully painted house. "They have real grass in their yard, too."

"Yes," *Ate* Ana said. "Both father and mother are doctor. They very kind. They helping our family when *Totoy* having typhoid, and we not able to pay hospital bill."

"Do you think they'll let their little children come to our Bible Club?" Jenny asked.

"Most probably they will," *Ate* answered.

Finally, they finished going to every house on the block where there were children the right age. Many of the boys and girls had stood shyly behind their big sisters or house girls who came to the gates. Everyone had greeted the girls kindly and said their children would probably come.

"Well, how many should we prepare for, Ana?" Mom asked when they returned.

"It depend, Ma'am. I think most probably twenty."

"But didn't we give out more than twenty invitations?" Jenny asked. "Most families have several children, and they all said they would come. Oh..." She was remembering the ask-three-times-thing *Ka*

Tala had taught her. "Do we need to take invitations around again?"

"I think we not need," *Ka* Tala said, coming inside from the patio with a load of dry clothes. "The one that say 'probably.' They most probably not come. Maybe twelve come, maybe fifteen, Ma'am."

"Well, we'll prepare *merienda* for twenty-four," Mom spoke up. "It's better to have enough. Ana, as soon as you come to work tomorrow afternoon, I'll have you go buy what we need. Then you can get it ready by club time."

"I will, Ma'am."

"Now, Jenny, I better print out a few more memory verses then you and Angel can cut them for me."

By four forty-five the next afternoon when the Christian Ed. lady arrived, everything was ready. The dining room table had been moved onto the patio. Ana had neatly laid out a variety of individually wrapped packages of cookies and chippies. A cooler of juice and stack of paper cups were ready. A small vase of flowers, a tape recorder playing children's songs, and a Bible were also on the table. Inside the Bible were small pieces of colored paper with the memory verse on them.

Soon, several small children arrived, each accompanied by an older sister or nanny. *Ka* Tala greeted each one and invited them to have *merienda*. By five fifteen, sixteen children and six older girls were seated on chairs and benches around the patio. *Ate* Ana collected the cookie wrappers and empty cups in a small trash basket, and Jenny handed each person a memory verse.

Then it was time to start. The Christian Ed. lady began by teaching the children several choruses, using word and picture cards and taped music. After the singing, she introduced Jenny's mom, then it was time for *Ka* Tala to teach the Bible story.

As Jenny watched it all, she prayed for Angel and *Ate* and all the children. She knew many had never heard the truth before. Even if it wasn't on her birthday, it was still the best birthday present she could have had.

At the end, the Christian Ed. lady had the children sing again then she taught the verse. She told them if they said it from memory next week, they would get a prize. Then Bible Club was over. Everyone said good-bye to Jenny's mom and left.

Ka Tala went home, and Mom went into her study room to finish her homework. "Did you like Bible Club?" Jenny asked *Ate* Ana, as she helped her clean up.

"I like. I not hear story last time. I planning on attending to church with *Ate* Tala next Sunday."

"That's our church, too. Will Angel go?" Jenny asked, excitedly. "She would be in my class. And you could go with Angel if you want to, *Ate*. Some *ates* stay. Even my mother stays with Davy."

"Maybe I go with Angel."

"That's great," Jenny gave her a hug. She didn't know what else to do she was so happy.

"Our brother attend sister church. Every first Sunday they attend same church like you."

"You mean I've seen your brothers, and I didn't know it?"

"Most probably you see. Bobby say he see you. Vic not always attend still. Christian Ed. lady invite me to college-age class she teaching."

"Are you going to go to college, *Ate*?"

"Yes. I have plan. But if I not able have job still, the money not enough to support my need." The corners of *Ate* Ana's mouth turned way down, and her face showed a sad expression.

"Will you want to continue working for missionaries?" Mom asked, coming into the kitchen.

"I like, Ma'am. My plan to attend to college if I getting job."

"I'll talk to the missionaries who will be living in this house after we move," Mom said. "They have three or four children. If they don't already have house girls, I think they would like both you and *Ka* Tala to continue working like you have for us."

"Thank you, Ma'am," *Ate* Ana said, smiling at Jenny's mom. "Shall I start vegetable?"

"You can start the rice first," Mom answered, taking carrots and green beans from the vegetable bin in the refrigerator. "Did you set out a package of pork chunks to thaw, Ana?"

"There, Ma'am." She pointed with her lower lip to a plastic bag on a plate on the counter. "Ma'am, will new missionary have Bible Club to our place?"

"You mean at this house? I hope they will. It should be going well enough not to take much time away from their language study."

Later, just before bedtime, the family sat down together for devotions. Jenny told about *Ate* Ana's plans to attend their church, and Jenny's dad told about his first Bible study with Angel's father. "Who would have guessed a few short months ago, when we were so discouraged, we'd be talking about these encouraging things tonight?" Jenny's mom asked.

"Why do we have to move just when everything is getting so fun?" Jenny asked.

"You know we came to work with minorities, Jenny," her father said. "These people in town have good churches they can attend if they choose to, but many people in the mountains and jungles still don't have any way to hear the truth about God. They should have a chance to hear."

"I know," Jenny said. She'd heard all this before. "What about MK school?"

"Do you remember my telling you all about the year I went to an MK school?" Mom asked. "Everything they do is for the children. That's the only reason the school's there."

"I did like what the kids I met at conference told me about it," Jenny added.

"Your dad and I are sure you'll do fine," Mom continued. "We know the dorm parents and trust them to take good care of you. Also, the family moving in here asked if we could stay for a few days after they arrive, so we could help them a little. I heard that one of their children would be going to that school. Maybe you'll have a friend to go with you."

"How old is she, Mom?"

"I don't know their children, Jenny."

"We think you've grown up a lot this year, Jenny," her father said, pulling her over against him on the couch and giving her a hug. "I really liked the way you worked to get this Bible Club going, and remember how you helped us give Angel's family a nice Christmas? It was an encouragement to all of us. It really was. I don't want to make you proud, but your mother and I are proud of you."

Jenny could not think of anything to say. It had been a busy day. She just smiled.

Gradually the night-parties stopped. Then one morning Jenny looked out her window and saw Angel. She was wearing a neat, navy blue and white school uniform. Her new backpack was swinging back and forth as she skipped to the corner. While she stood waiting for a *trike,* she looked up at Jenny's window. The two friends, who shared the same birthday, waved at each other. Jenny was sure that Angel knew she was happy for her.

As each week passed, Jenny tried to imagine what it would be like to go to MK school. Then one day, when she went up to her room after breakfast, she found the empty cardboard packing box sitting in the middle of her floor. She remembered packing her things in it to bring to the Philippines, but that seemed so far away and so long ago.

"Jenny," her mom called from her bedroom. "You need to start packing today. I'm gathering one suitcase full for each of us, and the rest will go to Manila on the truck that brings the new family's things here on Monday. I wonder if I should keep some of your things with us rather than sending everything to school with you."

Jenny wondered if she was supposed to answer. Didn't her mom know?

GOOD-BYE

Everything was almost packed when the truck pulled up in front of their gate around noon on Monday. Jenny couldn't wait to see the girl who was going to MK school. One by one the family piled out. But Jenny saw only small children—more Davy's age—being handed down from the high cab. She was puzzled.

Then she noticed people climbing down from the back of the truck. She saw a boy. Had the girl ridden in the open back as well?

"Hi," Jenny greeted the boy. "Where's your sister?"

He looked surprised. "You know my sister, too?" he asked. "She stayed in Manila with her friend."

"Oh," Jenny said sadly, starting to turn away, but the boy was still speaking.

"My sister already knows somebody else over here," he said quietly.

"What?" Jenny asked, confused.

"Nothing."

Noticing his questioning face, she "I remember when I first came, I didn't know anybody either. But you'll make new friends, except..." Jenny realized that she didn't know any boys nearby. Maybe Angel's brother... "There is one boy. His sister is my best friend. She lives over there." She looked toward Angel's house and pointed with her lip. "But Bobby doesn't live with them—"

"It's OK," the boy interrupted. "I won't be staying here anyway."

"I wanted to leave, too, when I first came," Jenny said, "but now I wish I didn't have to."

She tried to think of what else to say. How could she help? "When you get used to—"

"My parents are staying here," he interrupted again, "but I'm going to MK school."

"Oh, I thought it was your sister who was going," Jenny said.

"She's too old to go to the school where I'm going. My school only goes through eighth grade, and she's in high school. Her school is in Manila. Mine isn't."

"Oh," Jenny said, finally understanding. "You're the one! All the time I thought you were a girl."

The boy wrinkled up his nose as if he couldn't think what she meant.

"My mother said one of the children in your family was going to the same MK school I'm going to, so I'd have a friend to go with. I didn't know you were a boy... But we can still be friends," she added quickly.

"You mean you go to that school?" he asked, showing interest for the first time.

"I haven't been there yet, but I'm going soon."

"Do you want to?" he asked.

"I'm not sure," she answered honestly, "but my mom said everything they do there is for the kids. Sometimes I even feel a little excited about it. Some kids I saw at conference told me it's fun."

Just then she heard her name. "Come on inside, Jenny," Mom called from the door. "*Ka* Tala has dinner on the table. Is Daniel there with you?"

Jenny looked at the boy. "Are you Daniel?" she asked, knowing he must be. "Let's go in. You'll think the food is different, but it tastes good. Really."

Daniel smiled for the first time and followed Jenny inside.

As soon as they'd eaten, the men unloaded and reloaded the truck and took off. Their dads would return on the bus late that evening after delivering everything to a temporary storage place at the mission home in Manila. Davy and Daniel's two small brothers were put down for naps. Jenny had nothing left for her and Daniel to play with, but his mother found a couple games in one of their boxes as she started unpacking.

When *Ate* Ana came to work later that afternoon and saw Daniel, right away she asked, "How old are you?" When he told her he was ten, she said, "Almost same like our brother, Bobby. He want being friend to American boy. Next time I bring."

Daniel smiled at her uncertainly. Jenny guessed he was thinking he would not know what to do. "Don't worry," she told him. "After you are friends, it's just the same as being friends in the States."

That night was like camping out. All of Jenny's family slept in her room, so Daniel's parents could set up their own bedroom. Daniel and his two brothers slept in what used to be Davy's room.

In the morning at breakfast, Jenny found out they would be having their good-bye party the next day.

"We wanted to wait until you came," her mom was saying to the new family. "That way you could meet the teachers from the language school and a few people from the church."

"Will Angel's family come?" Jenny asked.

"Ana knows about it," Mom answered. "By the way, Jenny, you'll be glad to know that *Ate* Ana and *Ka* Tala will be continuing to work here after we leave, and that the Bible Club will keep going, too."

"Oh, good," she said, happily. "And what about *Ate* and Angel's father?"

"A man at church is taking over my Bible study with him," Dad answered. "He's met with us the last couple times. I'm hoping that when Jo Jo gets to know this man better, he'll start attending services with his girls. He told me he wants to."

The next afternoon, Angel sat very close to Jenny all during the good-bye party. "You will come back still?" she asked.

"I will, I promise," Jenny said.

"*Ate* say we not pray anymore to Mary. We know Jesus only one who already pay for all our sin," Angel said, smiling. "We happy now when we attending to Bible Club and our church."

Jenny squeezed the small brown hand lying on her arm. She couldn't speak the mixed-up thoughts she was feeling. Tears of sadness about leaving and uncertainty about living away from her family were ready to spill down her cheeks.

Then Jenny felt soft patting on her arm. She heard Angel saying quietly, "You going to be OK, Jenny... I praying for you."

Angel was going to be OK, too, Jenny knew.